He flipped the cigar butt into the leaping white water of the racing creek.

A few quick strokes of his knife and the sack of gold was free of the packframe. Slocum picked it up. It was a heavy son of a buck.

Something that felt like a hard-thrown brickbat smashed into the side of his head.

He felt his knees buckle.

He knew he was falling. He fought against it, trying not to go down, but not even sure why he should care if he fell or not.

He heard a second gunshot. *Second?* he asked himself. That seemed right, although he did not now remember having heard the first. Then he was falling forward . . .

OTHER BOOKS BY JAKE LOGAN

JAKE LOGAN

HIGH COUNTRY HOLDUP

BERKLEY BOOKS, NEW YORK

HIGH COUNTRY HOLDUP

A Berkley Book / published by arrangement with
the author

PRINTING HISTORY
Berkley edition / February 1984

ISBN: 0-425-06843-9

A BERKLEY BOOK ® TM 757,375
Berkley Books are published by The Berkley Publishing Group,
200 Madison Avenue, New York, N.Y. 10016.
The name ''BERKLEY'' and the stylized ''B'' with design are trademarks
belonging to The Berkley Publishing Group.

PRINTED IN THE UNITED STATES OF AMERICA

1

It was time to leave Durango. The whiskey was good and the ladies willing, but for the past few days Slocum had been getting an uneasy feeling.

There was nothing definite he could pin it on. Perhaps the pair of cold-eyed prospectors who had drifted into town with tales of hard luck and with well-cared-for Sharps rifles in their scabbards.

Not that he was afraid of them. John Slocum feared damned little and would back away from even less. But a man who is down on his luck will sometimes take desperate chances, and no one, including John Slocum, was immune to the impact of a heavy-caliber rifle slug fired into his back.

If those prospectors knew that there were wanted posters out on Slocum—which was all too likely, considering the number of the flyers still in circulation—they just might make their try. If they did, win or lose, it would inevitably be Slocum who would lose. If he died he would lose. If he lived he would lose in another way, because there would almost certainly be yet another want out with his name on it, if only because he could no longer afford the luxury of hanging around to answer questions and clear himself whenever trouble came up. Once he came to the official attention of the law in one place, there were simply too many others who would want to place their claim against him. Once behind bars here he was entirely too likely to be manacled and sent elsewhere.

More, Slocum was becoming plain weary of the constant vigilance that his loose and free way of life required.

He was tired. He wanted to rest. Settling down seemed out of the question for him. The habit of moving on had become too deeply ingrained, the wanderlust too strong. But a time, even if no more than a few months, when he could ride and move and enjoy the living without having to watch his back—that would be a joy and a relief. That much he longed for.

So he swallowed a last whiskey and saddled the Palouse horse he had picked up in a poker game down in Farmington and swung into the saddle. The hell with those two with their long rifles and empty pockets. If they wanted trouble they were going to have to come looking for it. Slocum was not going to give them any excuses or opportunities.

"Going somewhere, John?"

Slocum stiffened, then relaxed as he saw who had asked the question. This man was no threat, just an acquaintance from across a green felt covered table. "Telluride," Slocum said easily, although he had given no thought at all to where he might go next. Telluride would be as good a direction as any other.

The man nodded. "I'll miss taking your money tonight."

Slocum grinned. The play so far had gone quite the other direction. That was one thing about gambling losers, though; most persisted in wanting a chance to get their money back. And more often than not, a man who could be taken once could be taken twice. They always seemed to blame Lady Luck instead of their own poor knowledge of the odds involved, even though the Lady only seldom participated in a game.

Slocum nodded a brief goodbye and turned the spotted horse north toward Telluride.

"John."

"Yeah?"

"Ride careful. I've heard some talk. Liquor talk, I'd say, but it never hurts to be watchful."

"I always am. But I thank you for speaking out." This time Slocum touched the brim of his hat to the man—he could not even remember the fellow's name—in a silent salute before he bumped the Palouse into a trot.

He felt bad about not being able to recall the friendly man's name. He was genuinely touched by the warning. They were not friends, yet the man had gone out of his way to make a statement like that in this close-mouthed country where a man was expected to take care of himself or go belly-up without lament. Delivering the warning had been a kind and an unexpected thing for him to do, and Slocum truly appreciated it.

He rode north beneath the abrupt bluffs that surrounded Durango, thinking about the effects of human kindness.

He also kept a damned wary eye on his back trail, stopping frequently to examine the dusty track behind him.

There was dust back there, but whether from two men on horseback or from wind devils raised by the chill spring winds he could not decide.

"What do you think, horse?" he asked the Palouse as he pulled out a cigar and thumbed a match aflame.

He grinned wryly as he released a plume of blue smoke into the breeze. "It's hell, horse, when a man starts talking to a dumb beast. Says something about the dotty son of a bitch, it does. An' if you repeat any of this to a living soul, I'll have your gizzard for supper."

He thought about laying up for a while in ambush to find out for sure if the pair was on his heels, but reconsidered and rode on. If he faced them he would surely have to kill them, and then he would have brought on himself all the trouble he was trying to avoid.

Muttering curses at the two men who might or might not be behind him, he put the Palouse into a lope and moved more quickly up the wagon road to the north.

Telluride, he had said back there. Not a bad place. He had been there before and liked it. But having spoken of it now, he was not going to go there again.

He reached Hermosa Creek and splashed across the ford. The creek was running deep and swift, swollen at this time of year by the snowmelt. Durango lay in a sere and nearly barren pocket of rust-colored rocks and hills, but the country all around was wet and greening. The streams and rivers in this well-watered country were at or near their highest now.

On impulse, Slocum took the Palouse up the road a quarter mile, then let it drift off the wagon-rutted track as if of its own accord.

As soon as the Palouse's hoofprints were out of the easily marked dust, Slocum turned it and rode back along the verge of the public road, back to the swift run of Hermosa Creek.

The horse tried to balk about staying in the water, but Slocum forced it upstream, away from the road. The creek bed was rocky and the footing poor. The horse stumbled frequently, but Slocum held it in the water until they were several hundred yards from the road, then took it up onto the bank and hurried forward until he was completely out of sight from the road behind a hill that Hermosa skirted on its flow into the Animas River.

"That feels better," Slocum said aloud. The Palouse

flicked its ears in response to the sound of the man's voice.

He thought about circling back to see if the down-and-out prospectors—or anyone else, for that matter—might be following, but decided that the risks of being seen were more than the risk of being followed at this point.

He bumped the horse back into a trot and followed the creek north and west.

He camped that night in dense, black timber beside one of the many tributary creeks that fed the larger stream.

The spot was a good one. Thick timber and a spreading bog protected his back, and the site was set in a high bowl with steep hillsides all around.

It was obvious that the area was seldom visited. He jumped a herd of cow elk, ponderous with unborn calves, when he rode into the bowl. The elk had moved off to the north, the noise of their passage loud through the heavy growth, telling him two good things as they left. One was that no one was likely to move through that timber without noise. The other was that there almost certainly had to be a saddle or some form of exit from the bowl to the north. In the morning he would follow and leave by a route different from the one he had taken to reach the camp.

He built a small fire under the thick branches of a spruce. The dry aspen wood gave off practically no smoke, and what there was was dissipated by the spruce. As soon as his meal was cooked, he kicked the fire apart. The coals would be enough to keep his pot of coffee hot much longer than he would want to stay awake.

Slocum sighed and used one of the coals to light a cigar. He looked around.

This was handsome country, but damned lonesome. Slocum had never been the kind to depend on others for his entertainment—except, perhaps, for a woman when one was available—but relied on himself and no other.

Still, if come morning the Palouse fell with him and busted him up, there would be no one to know or to care.

If Slocum died now he would have left nothing behind. Not even friends.

Being missed would be scant legacy from a man's lifetime. But it was more than John Slocum was likely to leave. A man who travels where he can hear the owls hoot leaves nothing behind him when he goes under. Slocum knew that and had always accepted it.

He jumped damn near a foot off the log where he was sitting.

An owl's mournful hoot sounded practically over his head, startling him in his reflective mood. The big, pale-bellied bird was gliding silently overhead on the cool air of the early evening.

Slocum grinned up at the bird and shook his head at his own stupidity. It was only when he went to scratch his crotch that he realized he had unconsciously pulled his Colt when the owl hooted. The revolver was still in his hand.

Getting old, he decided, *but not necessarily real slow.* He uncocked the single-action Colt and holstered it.

There had been something tickling the back of his thoughts for some time now. He brought it out into the open and gave it a deliberate look.

In this country a man could be just about anything he chose to be, rough or smooth, either one. He could chance the luxury of a friendship or he could go his own way. He could even carry any name he might choose.

A man could change his ways if he wanted to. He was no more, and no less, than he showed himself to be.

A man could make a living, too, at any task he was

capable of performing. This was a country of wide-open opportunity.

John Slocum could not imagine himself tied to a farm or unlocking the doors of some damn store or saloon each and every morning of a dreary life.

But there were other ways that a man could get along.

Up here in this high, handsome country there were ways a man could keep on the move and still make his way.

Beef, for one thing. The mining camps—and they were everywhere in this country—were in constant short supply for beef.

A man could go into business for himself. Buy cattle down in the flatlands, say, and drive them into the mountains to sell at a profit.

The cattlemen did not pay attention to that need because so few animals were needed at any given camp and so few could be driven at a time in country so rough. But one or two men who could handle themselves could make out pretty well by driving no more than twenty or thirty head at a time and selling them here and there, then going back down to the low country and doing it all over again.

There would be risks. Inevitably there would be some beeves lost to falls off the trail or by escape into the black timber. But every animal delivered and sold would mean a fair profit.

Still, in order to make that profit, the drover would have to own his beeves outright. If he went partners with some flatland rancher, the profits would be halved or worse.

The only way to work it successfully would be for a man to have enough of a stake on hand that he could buy the cattle outright, assume all the risks himself, and pocket all the profits himself.

Slocum drew smoke from another cigar into his lungs and tongued the clipped end of the stogie. He knew what he had in his pockets. It was enough to gamble with. Enough to resupply when he felt the need. Enough to treat a woman or pay for a whore.

It was not enough to begin a venture of the kind he was thinking of now. It was not enough to let him get away from the constant threats of wanted posters and of fools who wanted to build their reputations by taking out the outlaw John Slocum.

He got his blanket from the bedroll behind his cantle and draped it over his shoulders, Indian fashion. When he sat down again he sat on the ground, using the log as a backrest while he finished the cigar and tossed it onto the softly glowing bed of coals left from his supper fire.

This country where he was right now was not too far as the crow flies from a mining camp he remembered called Howard's Tailings.

He had been there before, but in the company of men he did not trust worth a shit, and had never been back.

If a man wanted a stake, though, and if the outfit he had in mind was still producing gold, and if Howard's Tailings had not yet become a ghost camp like so many others . . . well, there was a way there that a man just might be able to work alone and get that stake put together.

It was a one-man opportunity Slocum had seen there, and there were damn few of those around. A chance for a quick hit and a quick out, with no one even the wiser until the deed had been done.

That was another nice thing about it. Done the way Slocum envisioned the job, no one would even know who had hit the concentrate shipment nor exactly when or where.

He thought about swollen Hermosa Creek and the way the snowmelt had all the streams in the area running full.

Even that was exactly the way it had to be for this job to work out.

The trail into Howard's Tailings was one of those eyebrow affairs carved out of hard rock and barely wide enough to accommodate a mule with a single pack balanced high on the packsaddle. There was not even room enough for a mule's panniers to be slung to either side, it was that narrow.

Slocum had ridden it once, and he had noticed that there were several cuts in the wall beside that trail, cuts where the mountainside dipped back away from the lie of the manmade trail, where water should be running now. They had laid pipe there and covered it with planking to keep the trail from being washed out every spring.

A man could leave his horse somewhere else or turn it loose and walk up the trail.

He could climb up into one of those cuts and lie in wait.

The concentrate shipments were heavily guarded, of course, but on that narrow, one-way trail the guards rode ahead of the pack train and behind it.

A man who was hiding in one of those cuts could wait there until the lead guards had passed and slip down to the narrow trail afoot.

He could cut the pack lashings as a few of those mules picked their way past him. Hell, he could cut as many or as few as he thought he could manage, and tip the packs over the edge of the trail. Just let them fall free to roll down into the canyon below.

Then he could let the mules, free of their burdens, go on their way behind the unsuspecting guards.

He could slip down off the trail and scramble down after the fallen gold packs. Slocum had looked. There were handholds enough that it could be done in a good many places, particularly where the water coming out of those cuts had gouged a way for him to get down.

Once he was down below at the canyon bottom, he could have a raft waiting, and load the gold onto the raft. The thing would not have to be large enough or sturdy enough to carry a man, too; he could work it with ropes from the bank, let the water and the raft do the job of carrying the gold off, and get away afoot and unseen by any of the guards.

When the shipment guards got to the other end and discovered the loss, the man could hide down below, offload the gold and hide it too, and let the raft drift free to be found empty miles downstream from where it had been released.

Whenever the guards quit their search and left the trail above—or at night, if they were persistent—the fellow could cobble up another raft and take the gold on out of the canyon. Raft it all the way down to the Dolores River or pack it out, whatever seemed convenient.

It should all be smooth and easy, Slocum figured, and no one would ever have seen who pulled the job, so there could be no wanted flyers out afterward.

It was as close to being free money as Slocum had ever heard of, and he was sure it would work.

He would have pulled it before except for the company he had been keeping at the time and the fact that then the water had been too low. Water enough to carry the raft was not likely to be a problem now.

And with the kind of stake a job like that would bring in undivided since he would be the only one in on it or even with any knowledge of it, he could, if he wanted, do some serious thinking about this business of supplying mining camps with fresh beef. He would have stake enough to buy a whole damned herd of beeves.

It was an interesting thought, he decided. Worth going over some more.

He could work in the open, under his own name or any other, yet still be on the move through open country, be just as free as he was now, but have a way of making an honest living at the same time.

It was interesting, he thought. He was still thinking about it when his head tipped forward and he slipped into sleep.

2

The road to the Howard's Tailings trail was much as Slocum remembered it. He was pleased to see that the ruts were fresh and there were fresh mule and horse droppings between the ruts, indicating that the road—and therefore the mining camp—was still very much in use.

The road came down from the north, winding its way through rocky spires and thick forests, to the rim above the gorge where a clever man with a raft could make his stake. That was another of the attractive things about the terrain. In order for a man on horseback to get down to the creek he would have to make a loop through the mountains of twenty-five miles or more to reach the Dolores and then double back into the gorge.

The road of necessity ended in a broad bowl, almost a valley, where wagon travel became impossible and the eyebrow trail took over.

Apparently there was not a great deal of traffic on the trail, because there was no permanent inn or saloon there, but a shelter of sorts had been erected since Slocum was last this way, and a stout corral had been built. Probably, he thought, the crude hut and corral were used by teamsters and their stock when they came here to meet mule packers from the camp.

Anything going into Howard's Tailings would have to

be transferred to mule packs here. Any goods coming out, gold concentrate for instance, would be shifted from the mules to the more efficient wagons for further transport.

Any really bulky equipment like boilers or furnaces simply could not be taken in over a trail that narrow, so it was almost certain that the Howard's Tailings mines would still be shipping raw concentrate instead of gold bullion. There would be no way to refine the metal without the proper equipment. Also, few mining camps were thought permanent enough to justify more than a simple stamp mill or two. Entire communities might disappear overnight when veins played out, so refining was usually left to major, well-established cities. As a result of that, though, the bulky concentrate was as easily negotiable in this country as pure placer gold used to be.

Slocum nodded with some satisfaction as he took in the details that all matched his memory. With any luck . . .

He took the Palouse to the start of the trail and stopped the animal to let it look at what was to come. Reaching this point had taken several days of circuitous travel through country that was steadily steepening as they moved slowly north and west, but so far he had not had to ride the Palouse over really treacherous ground like this promised to be.

The horse snorted and rolled its eyes at the look of the narrow trail, but it moved forward willingly enough when Slocum touched it lightly with his spurs. He was not so familiar with the Palouse that he would spur it hard when a misstep could become a disaster.

Within a few yards, man and horse alike were committed to the passage. From here on there was no room to turn around until they reached the first of the cuts where Slocum would be able to hide when the time came. Slocum did not want to think about what would happen if they encountered a pack train on the trail between cuts.

The Palouse was nervous but steadied as the time and distance on the narrow trail, nothing more than a rough-hewn ledge cut in the gray rock, increased.

They reached the first cut, and Slocum pulled the Palouse to a stop and dismounted to let the horse rest and calm itself further. Here there was room to turn or to pull aside if someone else might be coming. There was also opportunity to examine the cut for possible places to wait when a gold shipment was being made.

The cut sloped back from the trail at a steep but climbable angle. Water-slick rocks were at the point of the vee that had been cut into the side of the mountain here to form the natural cut, but its sides were lined with brushy growth that was just now beginning to leaf out into green foliage. To the south and at lower elevations the country was already greening, but this high the aspen were just starting to bud and the smaller growths were little more advanced.

A few more days, Slocum saw, and there would be enough green growth on those steep sides to help hide a man who did not want to be seen by passing guards. The rocks were small enough to serve as ladder steps, and the brush would help.

This first cut, Slocum thought, would be a suitable place for the job, except that being closest to the wagon road it would lead to the earliest discovery of the theft.

He mounted the Palouse and rode on again.

The second cut—he thought he could remember three— was another vee with its point cut into the mountainside. Here, though, the angle was too steep and the cut too shallow to permit comfortable climbing, and there was no screening brush to hide in. A man hiding here might well escape detection simply because he would not be expected and not looked for. But if seen he would have no route of escape and could be shot off the steep rock face with ease by any guard worth hiring.

If the third cut was no better than this, Slocum decided, he would have to go back to the first for his plan and accept the inevitability of a quick discovery.

In all, the trail was nearly four miles long and had to be covered very slowly. It was, Slocum realized, a seemingly impossible feat of perseverence and engineering, but it had been accomplished.

Nearly anything, it seemed, was possible when there was gold at stake.

Four miles of hacking through hard rock to create this thin excuse for a trail. Now there was even talk of bringing a narrow-gauge railroad into the San Juans. Slocum did not think it could ever be done, but there were men who were discussing the project with complete sincerity and with capital to back their dreams.

One thing was sure: the first man to drive a railroad into the high country would have his fortune assured, no matter what it cost him to get it there. And railroads had already been built into areas that Slocum would have thought impossible if he had not seen the completed work.

The men who truly amazed him with their energy, though, were the prospectors whose finds led to these later feats.

He had seen mine shafts drifted into cliff faces where steel ladders and steam hoists were needed to reach the tunnels. Working a shaft like that would have been hard enough. But *finding* a vein opening on a sheer cliff face would have required a level of industry that Slocum could scarcely comprehend.

He rode on, his thoughts running idly. The Palouse

seemed reasonably comfortable now, and Slocum had long since told himself to refuse to think about what would happen if the horse balked or took a false step.

He was approaching the third and last cut now, about a mile from the end of the narrow trail, when all hell broke loose.

Ahead he saw a flicker of movement and a gray, flowing shape.

It might have been one of the big cats that inhabited this country but were seldom actually seen. It might as easily have been some scurrying rodent, which was far more likely in broad daylight.

Whatever the cause, the horse obviously saw the same small motion.

Perhaps it smelled a cat. Perhaps it simply spooked. Slocum would never know, or care, which had happened.

The horse's ears flattened against his head and with a squeal of terror it reared.

Aw, shit, Slocum thought. There was no *room* here for a horse to act up.

The Palouse pawed at the air and edged backward, balanced on its hind legs.

Slocum kicked free of his stirrups and levered himself over the cantle of his saddle to slide free down the horse's rump. He felt the quick fear rise bitter as bile in his throat.

He fell clear of the horse and reeled backward, flailing his arms and grabbing at the slick rock wall beside him in a vain search for a handhold.

Off balance, he sprawled backward onto the narrow ledge of the trail.

Only feet away, the Palouse came back down to all fours. Its hind, off hoof skittered over the edge of the rock, and the animal panicked.

It tried to fling itself backward, and a hock rammed into Slocum.

Even then it might have recovered and remained on the trail, he thought, except that in its mindless terror the horse equated safety with the firm footing far to the rear.

It tried to spin around and race back in that direction, but there was no room for it to turn.

Slocum was trying to get to his feet. The horse in its thrashing slammed into him again, sending him flying, as it turned and planted its feet far out over the edge of the dropoff.

The horse was gone. And Slocum, off balance, tried to throw himself flat on the ledge.

He was too late. Too far off balance.

He grabbed for the edge, but his arm plunged down after the fallen Palouse.

He had no purchase on the slick rock. He grabbed with his right hand and felt his nails tear, but there was nothing to hold onto, nothing to grab.

He hit something hard, and he thought he could feel a rib shatter.

Then he was falling free.

There was nothing below him now but distant rock.

3

Slocum came to slowly. His head hurt and he thought he must have been unconscious for some time, but he was not sure about that. He was not sure about much of anything except that he hurt all over.

His head and ribs were the worst but hardly the only injuries. He ached everywhere, and his vision was foggy. Things seemed dark. He could not quite decide if it was his eyes or the time of day that made things seem dark and fuzzy. Possibly a combination of the two, he decided.

He shook his head, trying to clear his vision. That was a mistake. Waves of fresh pain washed through him.

Still, the sudden attack of sharp pain brought him fully conscious. He had not even realized until then just how groggy he was.

He tried to sit up and almost fell again.

With a surge of desperate strength, he grabbed onto the rocks where he lay. Fully aware now, he clutched at the rock and tried to figure out where he was.

He had fallen onto a jagged, protruding knob of rock on the cliff face where he had gone over.

Elsewhere along the trail, particularly below the cuts where he hoped to hide and make his play for some of the next gold shipment, it was possible to climb down to the creek and canyon bed far below. Here, though, the rock wall beneath the eyebrow trail was a sheer, sharp drop to the bottom.

He looked up, blinking. He must have fallen more than thirty feet to the point where he now lay, wedged precariously into the angle between the knob that had caught him and the face of the cliff.

Below him there was at least another hundred and twenty-five feet of rock and air before the stony canyon bottom was reached.

Slocum swallowed hard. If he had not hit this knob . . .

From where he was he could see the Palouse with his saddle, Winchester, and bedroll lying around it. The horse was obviously dead. Aside from the fact that nothing could have survived a fall like that, the animal's neck was bent back at a sickeningly impossible angle and dark blood stained the rocks at its head and rump. The horse had landed within feet of the swift-running creek. Even from so high up, Slocum could hear the cheerful burble of the racing water.

He swallowed again. His throat felt immensely dry, and a drink of that cold, clean water would be almighty good about now.

Without thinking about it, he began to lever himself off the knob where he lay.

Then he realized he had no way to get down. His rope was still on the dead Palouse's saddle.

He was not thinking clearly at all. Probably he had gotten a concussion when he fell. He shook his head again, but that only served to increase the pain.

It was apparent that he could not climb down to the creek level. There were no handholds or footholds that he could see at all on the rock face below. He would have to climb back to the trail and walk to the next cut before he might be able to crawl down.

With a grimace of pain, Slocum began reaching for handholds to pull himself up to the trail. He was not looking forward to the climb. Not the way he felt now— weak and dizzy and hurting all over—but it would have to be done.

Doggedly, he searched for a hold. Small protrusions, cracks, anything would do.

There was nothing. He could neither see nor feel anything that promised hope.

For the first time he realized that he was trapped here.

"Oh, shit," he mumbled aloud.

He closed his eyes and pressed his forehead against the cold, gritty rock.

The evening breeze was coming up, beginning to whistle down through the canyon now. It was cold. Slocum thought wistfully about the blankets and coat so impossibly far below.

He wondered—it was against his better judgement, but he could not control the thought—if he had finally, too late, taken that fatal misstep.

"Hello. Damn it, *hello!*"

The words rasped in his dry throat. It hurt just to speak, and he had to yell, trying to make himself heard.

He could hear the scrape of horseshoes on rock somewhere overhead. He was sure he was hearing that. Or almost sure. He had been almost sure of other sounds during the interminably long night he had just spent.

This time, though, he was certain he could hear horses moving above him.

It was several hours past dawn. Surely someone must be moving on the awful trail into Howard's Tailings.

He tried to yell again, but only a thin, ragged croak

issued from his throat. He coughed and spat and tried again. The results were little better.

"Hello up there!"

The hoofbeats continued uninterrupted.

Slocum wondered what he could throw up to the level of the trail to attract the attention of whoever was passing up there. It was not so far. Surely he would be able to throw something that far. If he had anything to pitch.

He thought of what might be in his pockets. If he could reach into a pocket to get anything. There were a few coins. Nothing bulky that might draw attention.

The hoofbeats were almost directly overhead now. A few more minutes and the travelers would be past.

It might be days before anyone used the trail again. Surely no one would casually ride that narrow ledge to and from the camp. No one sensible, that was sure.

Slocum felt around his aching midsection. His belt? Too light. His gun—that would do it. The Colt was big enough and heavy enough to carry for that distance. The Colt would do just fine.

He had it in his hand and was about to throw it when he realized his foolishness.

He was in worse shape than he had thought. He shook his head vigorously, welcoming the sharp pain that cut through the fog of his thoughts and brought him a step closer to reality.

He had a revolver in his hand, and he was about to throw the damn thing, when it would make all the noise he wanted.

Quickly he earred back the hammer and fired three quick shots in succession, the most common of all distress signals.

The gunshots seemed unnaturally loud, and his ears were already ringing from pain and dizziness.

Slocum was not completely sure, but he thought the hoofbeats above him slowed and then stopped.

Certainly he could hear nothing any more. Either the horses had stopped . . . or they had never existed to begin with. The sounds might have been a figment of his fevered imagination.

He raised the revolver to fire again, then thought better of it. Better to save the little ammunition he had in the Colt and in the loops of his gunbelt. His spare boxes of ammunition were down below in his saddlebags.

He craned his neck, trying to peer up to see if anyone was responding to the shots.

From where he lay, he could not begin to see any part of the narrow trail above. A hundred gold-laden mules might have been up there. The trail could as easily be empty of any form of life. He could not see, and now he could hear nothing either.

"Hello!" he tried again. The sound was so faint he could barely hear it himself. No one on the trail could possibly have heard.

Vast relief washed through him when he heard answering voices above. The voices sounded as near as if he was standing face to face with the unseen speakers.

"What was that, Burl?"

"Nothing, Mr. Rice. Just a hunter taking pot meat down below. Nothing to worry about. If you're ready to go on now—"

"Are you sure about that, Burl?"

"What else could it be, Mr. Rice? Has to be somebody huntin'. You know how sound carries in these canyons. Sometimes you can hear a guy talkin' half a mile off. You'd best lead on now, sir, or we'll be late for your dinner." There was the sound of laughter. "Reckon you don't wanta miss out on that, sir."

"I don't think . . ."

"It was just some hunter, sir. Go on now."

Slocum paled. If they rode on now . . . He fired the Colt again. He had only two cartridges left in the chamber, and he tripped them as quickly as he could, then reached immediately to his gunbelt to reload.

"Damn it, boys, I'm caught down here! Give me a hand up, will you?" He did not have strength enough to yell, but if sound traveled up as readily as it moved down they should be able to hear him.

"That sounded damned close, Burl. And I thought I heard a voice."

"Yes, sir, but—"

"Take a look, Burl."

"Yes, sir."

There was a pause and a series of scraping sounds. Apparently the man called Burl was getting off his horse.

Moments later Slocum could see the head and shoulders of a bearded man looking over the edge of the hanging trail.

"Here!" Slocum called. "Over here!"

"Well, I'll be damned!" The head and shoulders disappeared. "There is some yahoo down there, Mr. Rice. Reckon he fell off the trail an' got hung up on a rock."

Two heads appeared. There was the bearded man and beside him a much older and smaller man with silver hair and beard.

"Here!" Slocum yelled.

Both men saw him, and the older of them nodded. They were probably thirty-five yards away.

"Are you all right?" the older man called.

"I'm a hell of a lot better now than I was a little while ago. I been here since yesterday," he told them.

"We'll get you up. Hold on."

"I ain't leaving, believe me," Slocum told them.

The two disappeared and for an interminable length of time Slocum could hear scrapes and jangles and unindentifiable sounds issuing from above.

"Rest easy down there," one of the voices called at one point. "We're working on it."

Slocum had no idea what they might be doing up there. But whatever it was, he was for it.

After a while he heard the distinctive sounds of a hammer on metal. Soon afterward, a coil of rope snaked down over the edge of the trail.

The rope fell a good five feet away from him, and he groaned. There was no way he could reach it.

He saw the silver-haired man directly overhead. "It's all right," the man assured him. "We had to anchor the pins where we had a crack to work from. I'll bring the rope to you. Do you think you can tie yourself into it?"

"I reckon," Slocum answered. "I'd be able to climb it usually, but . . ."

"Don't try that, son. You might not be able to do it. Tie yourself into it and we'll pull you up."

"There's just the two of you?" Slocum did not think one old man and one younger man could haul him bodily up that face. There was certainly room for doubt, anyway.

"Don't worry about it. Now tie yourself into the rope."

The older man swung the hemp within Slocum's reach and leaned out, watching as Slocum pulled the rope around him under his arms and tied it securely in front of his chest.

"Take up the slack, Burl."

Slocum felt the rope tighten and then begin to dig painfully into his back. At least the pressure was above the ribs he assumed to be broken.

"Pull now, Burl."

Slocum felt the rope gouge harder, and then he was pulled up and away from the knob which had caught him.

He swung a few feet to the side and lost some skin on the abrasive granite. Then the lift was straight upward.

His head cleared the edge of the trail and he could see what the men had done.

A system of steel pegs with steel rings in their ends had been driven into the rock and a pulley hoist hooked onto them. The man named Burl was doing the lifting, while the older man directed the job.

The older man helped Slocum onto the narrow trail and Slocum collapsed there, as much from relief as from the pain he was experiencing all over again.

4

This time when Slocum came to, he was lying on level ground with a stand of huge aspen towering overhead. The man named Burl was tending a small fire while Rice sat nearby smoking a pipe.

"I thought you'd be around soon," Rice said. He was smiling.

"I owe you one," Slocum told him. He sat up but could not avoid wincing at the pain the effort cost him.

"Those ribs need to be bound, but we didn't have anything to do it with," Rice said. "There's a doctor of sorts back in Howard's Tailings. Not a regular doctor, but he manages mostly. He can take a look at you when we get you to the camp."

"Thanks." Slocum's nose wrinkled. "Is that coffee I smell?"

"Want some?"

"Sir, right now I'd drink anything."

Rice chuckled. "The coffee isn't ready yet, but I can give you some water." He got up and brought Slocum a canteen.

Slocum took several deep swallows and stopped drinking.

"It's all right, son. There's no shortage of water in this country. Finish it if you want."

27

"Thanks." Slocum drank again and this time nearly did empty the canteen.

"You look better," Rice said.

"I feel better."

"Good."

"I want to tell you how much I appreciate—"

Rice cut him short with a wave of his hand. "That's enough talk. It's all over and done with. We'll give you a bit to rest up, then go on to the camp. It's only a few more miles. Then you can find you a proper bed and get on with the business of healing."

Slocum nodded. "Whatever you say."

"I expect we could introduce ourselves," Rice said. "I'm Howard Rice. That fella over there doing the grumbling is my security boss Burl James. Burl gets suspicious any time there's anything unusual happening." Rice smiled. "Like finding a man hanging on the side of a cliff. That sort of thing makes him nervous, but I suppose that's what I pay him for."

James turned and nodded a curt hello that was definitely not friendly.

"Security boss? You aren't the man Howard's Tailings was named for, are you?"

"Oh, I guess that I am," Rice admitted.

"Then you own the mines there?" Slocum asked. The question drew a scowl from James.

"Not all of them," Rice said. "Just the one."

"The biggest one," James amended, "and the best."

"It isn't all that much," Rice said modestly. "Just some hard work followed by awful good luck."

"Did you make the original discovery here, then?" Slocum asked.

"Yes, I guess that I did. Came out first in the Pikes Peak rush and never had sense enough to quit. I spent my time working for wages in other men's diggings and took off on my own whenever I had a stake. After fourteen years I finally hit it.'' He grinned. ''Now I'm damn well enjoying it, too, son. Don't ever let anybody tell you different when they've got it made and are living on the high hog. It's fun.''

Slocum grinned back at the man. Rice seemed thoroughly to enjoy his good fortune now, after fourteen years of searching for his bonanza.

Slocum gave Rice a closer look. He was small, probably not taller than five foot four, and he looked to be at least in his sixties, but he was as lean as a rawhide reata and probably as tough as one under his genial exterior.

Burl James, on the other hand, was as large a man as his boss was small. James was built like a professional prize fighter and wore a pair of short-barreled Wells Fargo model Colts in cross-draw holsters high on his belt. He looked like he would be a hard man to deal with; there seemed to be no compassion in him. Slocum took a dislike to James, but he found himself liking Howard Rice very much.

Slocum sighed and reached for a cigar. He had two in his pocket and both of them had been crushed in the fall. He selected the largest and most whole of the four available pieces and lighted it.

''Mr. Rice,'' he said, ''I have something I need to tell you.''

''What's that, son?''

''I think I need to tell you how your operation could be robbed.''

Rice laughed, but James was instantly attentive. The security man looked angry as well.

''No reflection on you, James. Nobody can think of everything,'' Slocum said. ''But, like I said, I owe Mr.

Rice here, and I don't like to leave a debt unpaid." He took a puff on the cigar, having to hold the wrapper leaf together with his fingers to get the smoke to draw properly, and went on.

"My name is John Slocum," he said, "and I came here with the thought in mind of making my stake by taking some of yours. Here's how I figured to go about it. . . ."

Howard's Tailings had grown since Slocum last saw it. Apparently the smaller mines were still holding out, and Howard Rice's operation was doing very well indeed by the man's own admission.

Before, there had been only a few log structures in the camp. Now there were at least twice as many.

All of the construction had been done with native logs brought down off the surrounding mountains. Many of the smaller and less permanent-looking structures had been built with aspen logs. Those obviously had been put up by men who did not expect Howard's Tailings to last long. The logs were already warping and would not last nearly as long as the fir or spruce.

Rice's house was a huge affair built of fir. It likely would have been considered a mansion if it had not been made of logs.

"This is the place," Rice said proudly. "Help the man in, Burl. We'll take him to my study. He can sleep there for a night or two until it won't be so bothersome climbing the stairs to the bedrooms."

"Mr. Rice, I think—"

Rice cut him off. "I know what you think, Burl. You already told me what you think. I appreciate your opinion, but the decision is mine to make, and I've made it."

Slocum remained silent. Rice and his security man had been arguing the same point all the way from the trail-end to the camp. Howard Rice was determined to hire John Slocum for some special project he had in mind, and there was nothing that Burl James was likely to say that would change the old man's mind on the subject.

Whatever that subject was. So far, all Rice had told him was that he wanted to hire Slocum.

It would be, he had said, an alternate way that Slocum might get a stake put together.

Slocum did not particularly want Burl James's help getting from the pack mule to the big house, but he had to admit that he felt immeasurably weak and shaky after his overnight ordeal back on the trail. Still, pride could sustain him when his body could not. After only a step or two he shook off James's support and walked the rest of the way to the huge house.

"I'll take care of the animals, Mr. Rice," James said. "I'd like to come back and talk to you some more about—"

"I know what you want to talk about, Burl," Rice said. "We have already had that discussion. I will see you tomorrow at the digging."

James looked angry, but he stifled whatever he might have said and returned to the horses and mule.

Howard Rice led Slocum into the house and paused in the foyer to let his guest have a look at what the old man had built in this rugged, remote corner of the high country.

Slocum was impressed, as no doubt Rice intended.

The place was huge. The interior walls had been planed smooth and varnished to a bright gleam. There were lamps aplenty, Slocum noticed, but no chandeliers or anything else that could not have been transported on top of a packsaddle.

The furnishings were massive and looked masculine and comfortable. They, too, were built of native wood with pillows instead of upholstery for the seating. Another indication of the problems of supplying Howard's Tailings, Slocum thought.

Within those restrictions, though, Howard Rice had created for himself a comfortable and almost elegant home. The floors were polished to a rich gloss, and small rugs had been placed here and there to create a pleasant effect where carpeting might otherwise have been used.

"Mighty nice," Slocum said.

"Thank you." Rice pointed toward a doorway to their right. "The study is over there, John. Take that large chair with the footstool, and I'll bring you a drink."

Slocum walked painfully into the study but did not sit yet. "I can't have you waiting on me, sir."

Rice laughed. "Nonsense, John. I've climbed half the mountains in Colorado. Do you think I can't struggle across a room now to pour a man a drink?"

Slocum sat. It was easy to forget that this silver-haired old gentleman had had the endurance and the nerve to conquer an empty land in search of his fortune and to keep going until that fortune was made.

"Brandy?"

"I, uh . . . whatever you're drinking, sir." Slocum felt more than a little uncomfortable about receiving Rice's generosity after the admission Slocum had made to him. It was one thing to steal from a mining company. It was another thing entirely to think about taking something from a man who had befriended him. The idea of taking anything from Howard Rice now was repugnant.

Rice chuckled. He poured liquor from a decanter into two glasses and brought one to Slocum. He settled into a slightly smaller chair than the big armchair Slocum had been given.

"No doubt," he said, "you are wondering about this job I have in mind for you, John."

"I would say that it has crossed my mind, yes, sir." Slocum took a sip of the liquor. Instead of the relatively mild brandy he was expecting, it turned out to be an exceptionally smooth rye whiskey.

Rice saw his surprise and grinned. "I kinda figured you weren't much for a dandy's drink. Well, neither am I."

Slocum raised the glass toward the old man and took a deeper drink. It tasted mighty good.

"There's cigars in the box beside you," Rice said. "If you want anything else, ask."

"Yes, sir." Slocum reached for a cigar. A silver nipper and a box of matches were beside the humidor. The smoke was as mellow as anything he had ever tasted.

"About this job," Rice said. "You might be able to help me with something."

"Anything I can do, sir. I told you that I owe you. I don't say something like that real lightly."

"I never thought you did, John, or I might not have had this thought of mine since you told me who you are and why you came here. The first thing that I'd like you to do, though, is to quit calling me 'sir' and 'mister' and all that crap. My name's Howard. I'd like you to keep that in mind."

"Yes, sir. I mean, Howard."

"Good." Rice took a drink of the whiskey and reached for a cigar. "The thing is, John, I've been losing a fair amount of my gold."

Slocum's eyebrows went up.

"Burl is doing the best he can. He is absolutely beside himself with worry over it. And he does do a fine job of handling the high-graders. Every mine has that, of course. You try to pay a man a decent wage and still make your profit, but there's always some that figure they should be able to take home any good-looking chunks of ore they find. Like I say, you'll always have that, but Burl is doing a good job of keeping the high-grading losses to a minimum. But I'm convinced we have been having some other losses, much more significant ones, that neither he nor I can get a handle on. There have also been rumors reaching me from the outside that we are in line for a big robbery. Burl and I have worried over that for weeks, ever since the rumors got back to us, but I'm afraid someone else may have some ideas about a robbery, as you yourself did. And that is what I would like you to do for me, John."

Slocum was confused for a moment.

"I think with your fresh and shall we say, 'professional' point of view, John, you may be able to find our weaknesses and correct them before I am hit with a loss that I can't afford." Rice took another drink. "Most people don't realize it, John, but as a mine operator I have more to do than spend my money. Don't get me wrong, now. I make plenty and I do enjoy spending it. But in addition to what I take out of the mine, there are nearly a hundred men who depend on me for their livelihood. If I go under, so do they. And I will tell you quite candidly that every shipment I make out of here is required for me to continue operating. Payroll costs alone are enormous, and if I ever get caught in a cash flow problem so that I can't meet my payroll, I might as well shut down. Hard-rock miners work hard and they are entitled to every penny of their wages. I wouldn't expect them to react with anything but violence if I ever come up short of paying them what I owe."

That was a problem Slocum had never thought of before. His gut reaction was that owning a gold mine was something like being given free use of a U.S. mint. The only problem with money would be how to spend it all. But gold concentrate was not the same as money. It would have to be sold somewhere and converted to gold coin to meet a payroll. He wondered if Rice was correct about the miners' reaction if they ever failed to get their pay in the hard coin they demanded. Probably so. Paper currency or checks would not be accepted, even if Rice had the money in a bank somewhere.

"Anyway, John," Rice went on, "I would like you to look things over here and tell me if you can find the weaknesses in our security. As a special consultant, if you will. If you succeed, I will pay you a handsome bonus. Enough, possibly, to make that stake you were talking about. If not, you will be out a little time. Nothing more. Naturally I would expect you to stay here and get over your experiences before you go to work on this."

"You'd be willing to take me into your home after what I told you I was planning to do?"

"I believe you are a man of honor, John," Rice said mildly.

Slocum stared into his whiskey glass for a moment. "I used to be."

"I believe you still are," Rice said with confidence. "May I ask you a personal question?"

"Yes, sir."

"Your voice has the soft qualities of the South in it, and from your bearing I would say that you might once have been an officer. Is that correct?"

"That was a long time ago."

Rice smiled. "Not that long, John Slocum. Not so long that you would be willing to abandon honor. No amount of time is that long. I suspect I could not choose a safer person to entrust my gold to, once you tell me that you will accept the job I am offering."

Slocum drank from the glass and paused for a moment. "I accept the job, sir, and the conditions that implies."

Rice got the decanter and refilled both glasses. He raised his in a toast and drank. "I feel better about it already."

Slocum hoped Rice would never have cause to change that opinion.

5

"This is Mr. Slocum, dear. Lynnanne is my daughter, John."

Slocum came to his feet abruptly, surprise registering on his lean, tanned face. Rice had made no previous mention of having a family, but Slocum would have been in a state of shock even if the man had described this exquisite creature who had made her entrance into the dining room of the log mansion.

Lynnanne Rice was gowned and coiffed fit for Denver or even New Orleans.

Slocum swallowed hard and got control of himself. Quite automatically he bowed to her. It seemed the most natural thing to do.

The girl was lovely. Her hair, piled high and pinned into an elaborate confection, was raven and her eyes were a startling blue. Her complexion, covering high cheekbones that narrowed to a delicate chin giving her face a heart shape, was that of bone china.

She was small, barely five feet if that, and Slocum's lean frame towered over her. She offered her hand and he took it, bending to brush his lips near her soft, scented flesh without ever actually touching her except with the tips of his fingers. When she smiled there were tiny dim-

ples at the corners of her dainty mouth. She wore no
cosmetics, and she needed none.

"My apologies for my appearance, Miss Rice."

"There is no need, Mr. Slocum. Daddy told me you
were in an accident."

"Which reminds me, John, I'll send a man out tomorrow to climb down and get your gear. You won't be
feeling up to that for a while yourself."

"Thank you, sir."

"I can loan you a razor in the morning, so you should
survive."

"Yes, sir."

Rice smiled at him. "Howard. Remember?"

"Yes, sir."

Slocum helped the girl into her chair across the table
from his, then returned gratefully to the place he had been
given. He had noticed the extra place setting but had
assumed that Burl James or perhaps Rice's mine superintendent would be joining them for the evening meal. Now
Slocum wished he had been more careful about washing
and slicking his hair back before they ate.

As soon as they were all seated, whether by signal or
timing or mere chance, a door opened from the kitchen
and a young woman came in. The serving girl was dressed
in a neat, dark uniform and was quite pretty. She probably
would have seemed even more attractive except that her
measure of beauty seemed pale in comparison with Lynnanne
Rice's.

Howard Rice might have spent many years prospecting
in the high country, but somewhere along the line he had
managed to acquire expensive tastes.

Supper was a creamy onion soup followed by a roast
that Slocum thought might be elk along with potatoes,
white bread, gravy, and vegetables. Slocum was delighted

to find that there was not a bean to be seen. Probably Rice had had more than enough of those during his lean years. Dessert was a yellow custard that must have been made with eggs although Slocum could not imagine how they would freight eggs into a camp as remote as Howard's Tailings.

Lynnanne ate sparingly, and Slocum, as hungry as he was after going so long between meals, found his attention more on Howard Rice's captivating daughter than on the food. There was little conversation during the meal.

When they were done, Rice asked Lynnanne to excuse them and led Slocum back to the study for whiskey and cigars. Slocum hoped his host had not noticed his preoccupation with the girl. But as pretty as she was, there was just no way he could have avoided paying attention to her.

"To your good health and future success," Rice said, raising his glass toward Slocum.

"And to yours, Howard."

Rice finished his drink and his cigar quickly and stood. "I know you're tired, John. Why don't you go to bed now?"

"I've been thinking, Howard, and I don't want to deprive you of the use of your study. I can certainly climb a flight of stairs if you have a spare room upstairs, or I can go rustle myself someplace else to bed down."

"I won't hear of you going elsewhere, but if you are sure you feel up to the stairs . . ."

"That meal and drink have me fixed up just fine, Howard. I can manage."

Rice led him slowly up the broad staircase and showed him to a bedroom. The bed was made up with real sheets, a rare luxury, and the mattress was filled with down or feathers. Apparently Rice had spared no expense with the things it was possible to freight over the trail into Howard's Tailings.

Slocum stripped as soon as his host was gone and was asleep almost as soon as he felt the touch of the down pillow.

Slocum came awake instantly and swept the always-ready Colt into his fist. Something—he did not really know what—had disturbed his deep sleep and brought him into a state of taut readiness.

He heard the door to his bedroom close and the latch click. He had no idea who had just come into the room, but he drew the Colt's hammer back, muffling the telltale click with his free hand as the sear engaged.

A match flared brightly in the darkness, and he relaxed. He uncocked his revolver but did not yet lay it aside. The yellow glow revealed that for some reason Howard Rice's daughter Lynnanne had come into his room.

A mistake? Simple courtesy in checking on the health of her father's guest? Slocum decided that the best way to find out was to ask. "What are you doing here?"

The girl jumped slightly at the unexpected sound of his whisper. Her eyes widened when she saw the Colt in his hand, and she dropped the match she was holding. The rush of air as it fell extinguished the tiny blaze, and the room was again plunged into total darkness.

"Stay where you are," Slocum warned. "Don't move for just a moment, Miss Rice."

He reached to the bedside stand and found matches. He flicked one alight and lit the coal-oil lamp.

Lynnanne had not moved at all. She was still staring toward the bed and the big revolver.

"Something you should know, miss," Slocum said. "It ain't always a good idea to sneak in on a man who's traveled the empty places.'' He shoved the Colt back into its holster on the bedpost and pulled the sheet higher over his chest. He had gone to bed naked and did not want to offend the girl, whatever her reason for coming into his room. "Now," he said, "you might answer my question."

"Oh." Lynnanne blinked and visibly relaxed once the gun was out of sight. She smiled, but Slocum thought he could still detect a faint quiver at the corners of her pretty lips.

Whatever the reason for this visit, and whatever the hour, Lynnanne was obviously already prepared for bed herself. She was wearing a satin robe belted tight around a tiny waist, and her black hair was let down into a gleaming fall that came down as far as that delectable waist.

"Was there something you wanted?" Slocum asked.

This time the smile was genuine. And, incredibly, Slocum could see a certain quality in her eyes that he never would have expected to find there.

Her lids lowered, and she looked at him with a smokey sensuality that was anything *but* ladylike or genteel. The pink tip of her tongue licked out to play across her lips, and her eyes seemed to be fixed on a point just south of Slocum's midsection where a fading nocturnal erection continued to raise a hump in the bedclothes.

"Miss Rice?" Slocum was beginning to feel acutely uncomfortable, even embarrassed.

Lynnanne looked him in the eye and smiled again. When she spoke there was a quite unmistakable husky quality in her low voice. "Yes. There is something here that I want, Mr. Slocum."

"Look, Miss Rice, I think you should go back to your own room now." If he had not been naked, Slocum would have jumped up and escorted the girl out of his room, by force if necessary. There are certain things a gentleman simply did not do, and seducing the daughter of the man who had befriended and trusted him was right up near the top of that list.

Lynnanne gave him another of those heart-melting, groin-tingling smiles, and in spite of himself Slocum could feel that damned unwanted erection returning. The sheet below his waist popped up like he was trying to hide a tent pole down there and began to throb and bump in time with his heartbeat, which was considerably quicker now than it had been a few moments earlier.

"Oh, my, yes," Lynnanne whispered. "I would say that there is most definitely something here that I want, Mr. Slocum."

She started toward the bed.

"Wait. Now wait just a minute there, Miss Rice," Slocum said. He leaned down and pulled a blanket from the foot of the bed to help cover his all-too-obvious interest. That didn't really help, but he tried.

Lynnanne laughed. She reached for the bow knot that tied her robe closed and gave one end a gentle tug.

Slocum groaned.

She was not wearing anything under the damned robe.

The cloth parted and fell aside. Lynnanne shrugged her shoulders and let the expensive fabric slither lightly down to the floor.

Slocum swallowed and wondered frantically what the hell he was supposed to do now.

Probably the proper thing to do would be to refuse to look at her. Well, there were many things he was capable of, but turning his head right now was not among them.

Lynnanne had an extraordinary body. And all of it was right there for Slocum to see.

Her breasts were perfect, high and firm and tipped with unusually small and pink nipples. His hands would have fit around her waist with room to spare. Below that her hips swelled to a soft roundness.

Her pubic hair—Slocum blinked and stared in spite of his best resolve—she *had* no pubic hair. She was shaved as bald as a hard-boiled egg, the soft, flat planes of her belly narrowing to display a half-seen blush of pink at the lips of her pussy.

Pussy! *Damn* it, Slocum thought. It wasn't even right for him to *think* a word like that in connection with Howard Rice's daughter.

Her legs were slim and shapely. All in all, small as she was, she seemed like a perfectly proportioned china doll.

A warm, breathing, too obviously hot and ready china doll.

Lynnanne came toward him, her lovely eyes damn near smouldering as she stared at the insistent erection that continued to poke and prod at the bedclothes.

"Oh, my, yes, Mr. Slocum," she repeated in that husky voice, "there is most definitely something here that I want." She looked him in the eye and giggled, running her tongue over her lips in a slow, teasing manner.

Slocum groaned again and slid lower in the bed Howard Rice had provided for him.

"Miss Rice, please."

"Yes? Please what, Mr. Slocum?" She laughed and cupped her breasts in her hands, leaning forward to offer him the rosebud nipples.

"Go . . . away," Slocum croaked.

"You don't want me, Mr. Slocum?" She laughed again. "Or may I call you John? After all, you are a guest in my daddy's home. Perhaps I could call you John. And you could call me Ready."

She leaned farther forward, almost forcing her nipples

against Slocum's lips, and he could smell a faint, flowery fragrance on her skin.

Lynnanne laughed again.

Whatever effect she might have wanted from that, it was the release Slocum had been wanting. All of a sudden he was no longer looking at her with demanding lust. He was angry with her for acting like this, for dishonoring her father. For expecting John Slocum to dishonor the man further.

Slocum's erection sagged and disappeared. He sat upright in the bed and gave her a cold stare. "That's enough, Miss Rice. You've had your fun. You've teased and taunted enough. Go back to bed—alone, if you please—and let me sleep now."

"Why, Mr. Slocum, I almost believe you mean that."

"I do," he said coldly. "Get out of here."

She would not let it go, although she must have heard from his tone of voice that he meant the rejection. "Or what, Johnny? What will you do if I don't go?" She laughed and wriggled her hips, waggling the moist lips of her pussy only inches from his nose.

But Slocum was not looking there any longer. He was giving her a glare eye to eye, and his expression was hard and cruel now.

"Go back to bed, Miss Rice."

"You can't be serious, John. Surely . . ." She cupped her breasts again and let her hands trail lightly down her sides, outlining the narrowness of her waist and the delectable swell of her hips.

"Go."

Lynnanne sighed.

"Now," he said.

She pouted, but after a moment, finally willing to believe that he was actually turning her away, she turned and with neither coyness nor shyness walked back to pick up her robe and pull it on.

With the robe on and belted, her dignity aided perhaps by the covering, she turned back to him. With genuine curiosity in her voice she asked, "Am I that unattractive to you, John?"

"You know better," he said. He did not bother to explain further. If she did not understand the reason why he could not take her to bed, that was Howard's problem. John Slocum was not responsible for the damn girl's upbringing. "Good night," he said.

With a sigh, Lynnanne turned and let herself out of the room.

Slocum, damned well more awake now than he wanted to be, blew out the bedside lamp and tried to return to sleep. It was entirely too long before he was able to achieve that.

6

Lynnanne did not appear at the breakfast table the next morning. Whether she was pouting or simply sleeping in later, Slocum neither knew nor cared to guess. He was glad, though, that she was not there. It had been difficult enough having to reject her advances. Having to look at her, wanting her, while her father was in the same room would have been almost too much after the poor night's sleep he had been able to get after she finally left his bedroom.

Howard Rice certainly seemed happy enough, though, and must have slept very well indeed. He looked dapper in a business suit worn with a gold and scarlet vest and matching spats.

"Good morning, John," he said cheerily when Slocum answered the maid's summons and came down to the table set for two.

"Morning, Howard."

"I hope you slept well," Rice said with a twinkle in his eye.

"Passing fair." Slocum rubbed his freshly shaven chin and added, "It does feel good to get some of the bristles and dirt off. It was thoughtful of you to have the bath brought up. Thanks."

Howard nodded happily. "Anything for a guest," he said. "Particularly one who is a gentleman."

47

Slocum shook his head and accepted a most welcome first cup of coffee from the maid. "I reckon that would be stretching the truth some, but I thank you just the same."

The maid placed several heavily loaded platters onto the table and let herself quietly out of the room. When she was gone, Howard Rice's good humor erupted into laughter. "Oh, John, you . . ." He was laughing so hard he could not continue.

"What's so funny?" Slocum asked as he helped himself to huge portions of ham and biscuits and fried eggs. By now he had concluded that Rice brought hens into the camp instead of trying to freight fresh eggs in.

"You," Howard said, trying with limited success to stifle his laughter.

Slocum laid his fork back down and surreptitiously glanced down at his clothes to make sure he had not somehow spilled something all over his shirt or come to the table with his fly undone or anything equally ludicrous.

"Damn it, Howard, what is so funny this morning?"

Rice went into gales of laughter all over again. Slocum shrugged it off and began to eat his breakfast.

"John, I . . . oh." Rice stopped and used his napkin to wipe his eyes. He calmed a little and tried again. "I . . ." Too soon. The laughter got the better of him again. He sat in his chair, rocking back and forth, holding his stomach.

"Howard!"

"John, I . . . last night . . . it was so *funny!*"

Slocum gave him a look that clearly said he was wondering if the old fellow had gone suddenly daft.

Rice saw it and went into peals of fresh laughter. He pointed a shaking finger at Slocum and guffawed with loud, long brays that doubled him up and made him wipe his eyes several times over again. "You . . . you . . . Lord love you, John, you must have been so funny."

"What?"

"Last night. Oh." He got control of himself, wiped his eyes a final time, and sat upright in his chair taking deep breaths. "Oh, John, that's the finest laugh I've had in I can't tell you how long."

"I still don't know what's so damn funny," Slocum said. He spooned a dollop of blackberry jam onto a piece of biscuit and crammed it into his mouth.

"Oh, I'm sorry. Truly I am. Well, a little." Rice began to chuckle again. "And it wasn't done in fun, John. You should understand that. That wasn't the reason, anyway, even though it turned out to be so funny."

"Howard, I honestly do not know what you are talking about."

"I know that, John. That's what makes it so damn *funny*, you see."

"I appreciate a good ribbing as well as the next man, Howard, but what in the hell are you talking about?"

"You. Last night. My darling daughter." Rice began to laugh uncontrollably again.

Slocum felt himself go pale. He was about to stammer out something like a denial or an explanation. Or anything, except that he could not think of anything that would remotely excuse Howard Rice knowing about Lynnanne being in that bedroom last night. Then he stopped and clamped his mouth shut. Howard was *not* taking this the way Slocum would have expected once the old fellow found out the girl had been there. Not anything like what Slocum would have expected.

"Howard!"

Rice's fits of laughter died away again, and the man managed to look almost serious. "Oh, John. I am sorry to have put you through that, but it was a test of sorts. I was sure I knew what kind of man you are. I told you that last night. But I did want to verify that judgement. I am glad to know that you are precisely the man I thought you were, regardless of recent reputation.''

"Howard, I still don't know what the *hell* all of this is about.''

"Of course you don't, my good fellow.'' Rice chuckled a bit more and forced himself finally to quit laughing. "Oh, John. Lynnanne and you, last night.''

"I can assure you, Howard, that nothing . . .''

"Of course not. Of course it didn't. Don't you see, John? That's the entire point. That is what you proved. You are a man I can trust completely.''

"You sent your own daughter in to . . . ?'' Slocum was beginning to rise, ready to leave the table and the house and the whole damn camp of Howard's Tailings.

Rice, instead of acting insulted, was laughing again. "Sit down, John. Please. Give me a moment to compose myself. Oh!'' He dabbed at his eyes with the napkin and waved Slocum back into his chair.

Slocum remained standing, his napkin in his hand. About one more minute of this and he was gone.

"John, please sit. Please. Of course you don't understand yet. But, John, my good fellow, *I've never been married*.''

"What?''

"I said, John, that I have never married.'' Rice began to laugh again.

"But . . . ?''

"My dear fellow, I have no children.'' Rice chuckled. "None that I know about, anyway.''

"But Lynnanne . . .''

"Lynnanne's name is Duffy, John. Not Rice. She is my mistress.'' He gave Slocum a wink. "Quite a fetching little thing, wouldn't you say? Private property, of course, until I kick the bucket, but a delightful girl, all in all.''

Slocum felt like he had been kicked in the belly. Instead of a virgin daughter he was honor-bound to protect and stay away from, the damn girl was a wealthy gentleman's plaything who had been screwed probably a thousand times or more.

His first reaction was a surge of anger. Then Slocum, too, began to laugh. ''You son of a bitch, Howard, do you *know* the kind of night I spent after she left?''

Rice chuckled and nodded. ''Exactly the kind I would've if she had been allowed to stay there, I judge.'' He began to laugh again.

Within moments, both men were laughing heartily.

After a time Rice rang for the maid. ''Bring us a bottle of whiskey to go with this grub, Catherine,'' he told the girl. ''I think John and I need something to settle us down here.'' He began to laugh again, and the maid looked distinctly puzzled as she went off to fetch the bottle.

Slocum sat in Howard Rice's study with his feet propped up, a decanter of whiskey on one side of him and a humidor of fine cigars on the other. High living, he thought, but boring just the same. He was feeling better than he probably had any right to be and was in no mood to read month-old copies of the *Rocky Mountain News* from Denver.

Rice had gone off to his mine offices to do some work, leaving Slocum unattended in the house. John had wanted to go along and get to work on the old gentleman's security problems, but Rice refused to permit it, saying Slocum was in no condition for that yet and that there was plenty of time for him to recover before any more shipments were scheduled.

So Slocum sat and cooled his heels and tried to make

himself believe that a life of luxury was something to be desired. The truth was that Slocum was not the kind to sit around doing nothing, and an existence of leisure and wealth would probably only make him old before his time.

The study door opened and Lynnanne came in.

"What I ought to do," Slocum said, "is turn you over my knee and give you a sound spanking. That was an ugly thing for you to do to a person, you know."

She did not look particularly contrite. She laughed and gave him a lewd wink. "Daddy said he was going to tell you this morning. I take it that he did."

"Daddy? Don't you think it's time you dropped that?"

"Oh, I wasn't trying to be funny, John. Mr. Rice likes his ladies to call him Daddy. He also prefers girls who are on the small side. And I *know* you noticed last night that he likes his girls without, shall we say, excess hair." She giggled. "But you did *try* not to look. I will give you the credit that is due. You did try." She was laughing again.

"You aren't the only one, then?"

"I am the only young lady who *lives* here," Lynnanne said with some pride. "I am the mistress of the house as well as of the master. But Daddy does enjoy some variety in his appetites."

"You take that rather calmly."

"Shouldn't I? He is a very generous man, John. I am quite ready to please him in any way that I can. Jealousy would not please him; therefore, I have no jealousy."

"And if he wanted you to be jealous of him?"

Lynnanne laughed. "Then I would scratch out the eyes of any woman who looked at him."

"A lucky man, Daddy Rice."

"Thank you, sir."

Just looking at this pretty filly made Slocum's erection return. Not that he had been long without one ever since she left his room last night. The problem was becoming painful, as a matter of fact.

This morning, unfortunately, she was dressed. She was wearing a fresh gown that was cut delightfully low in the bodice and nipped in to a marvelously small waist. Her jet hair was once again done up in elaborate coils. Slocum remembered all too well what she looked like without the clothing and the hairdo.

A pretty thing, Howard Rice had called her. The old man had been damn well right about it. He had also mentioned that she was his own private stock.

"It's a pity I didn't know last night," Slocum said. He took his time about deliberately looking her over from head to toe, his eyes lingering on the half-moon displays of creamy breast visible at the front of her gown.

Lynnanne gave him a coy glance and asked, "And what would you have done if you had known, sir?"

Slocum took a sip of the whiskey and grinned. "Why, girl, I'd have fucked you until you were too sore to shave that pretty patch of yours again for a week or more."

Lynnanne looked at him and gave him another wink. "From the looks of that tool I saw last night, you might be able to do it, too."

"Try me."

"Is that a dare?"

"You bet it is."

"But Daddy told me not to."

"Do you tell Daddy everything?"

"*Almost* everything."

Slocum motioned her closer. He took his feet off the footstool and kicked it aside. He pointed toward his crotch, where by now his massive tool was trying to hammer its way out of his fly.

"I think I should be frightened of anything that big," Lynnanne said.

"Should be, maybe. Are you?"

She grinned and shrugged.

"After last night," he said, "you shouldn't expect a lot of sympathy from me."

"You do tempt me, sir."

Lynnanne dropped to her knees, taking the time to flounce the skirts of her gown and arrange them around her on the floor. Then with skillfully practiced fingers she slipped the buttons of his fly from their holes, and Slocum's cock sprang into view.

"Mmmm," she said. "So big and red and ready." She unbuckled his belt and slid his trousers down. Delicately she cupped his balls in one hand while with the other she stroked him gently. "This is really quite lovely, you know," she said.

Lynnanne bent forward. She held him with a light touch and ran the engorged red head of his cock across the softness of her cheek.

Slocum expected her to take him into her mouth. Instead she bent still lower until her right eye was near the extraordinarily sensitive head of his throbbing member. She fluttered her eyelashes. That faint, fluttering touch was maddening in its effect.

Slocum held her by the back of her head and pushed her gently down on him. She resisted just long enough to look up at him with a knowing smile of victory. Then she went where she was directed.

She was hardly a reluctant maiden. Nor was she merely going through the motions. She engulfed him with a strong, vigorous pull of lip and mouth and ran her tongue eagerly over him.

Slocum leaned back in the chair and shut his eyes,

letting the sensations wash through him the way he had spent half the night imagining she would be.

Her fingertips fluttered busily against his balls, and even though she had barely begun, Slocum could feel the rising surge of his come preparing to explode.

Slocum shuddered, and hot jism spewed out into her throat. He arched his hips and pounded into her, pressing the coarse, curly hair of his crotch against her nose.

Lynnanne stayed with him, continuing to suck and pull at him as long as he continued to pump come into her and staying even afterward to drain the last possible drop from him.

Finally, when the turgid insistence was gone, the last of his immediate pressures released, she withdrew slowly, stopping frequently to suck and lick, until finally he dropped free of her mouth to lie in her hands.

Lynnanne stood. She gave him a catlike smile as, provocatively, she licked her lips and wiped her mouth on the back of her hand. "All done?" she asked.

"Just beginning," he assured her. "Take your dress off."

"Surely you can't be serious," she said.

"Surely I am," he said. "Surely you can't have forgotten what it's like to be with a young man again."

"You aren't that young," she said.

"Try me."

A smile came into her eyes as she saw his pole rise once again to attention, and she began to work with feverish haste to undo the long line of buttons at her bodice.

Her dress was on the floor within seconds, and she stood gloriously naked in front of him. She was very small, and Slocum thought she looked more than a little nervous when she looked at him this time. But she seemed eager too.

She looked around, but there was no bed here or even a couch they could lie on. Slocum pointed to the floor.

She lay down and opened herself to him. The pale, smooth, shaven flesh surrounding the bright, wet pink of her sex gaped wide.

"Be careful," she said. "I don't know if I can take all that."

"You can," he assured her.

He was right.

Again and again and yet again he was right.

7

The maid called Slocum to lunch about one o'clock. Lynnanne had long since left the study, saying she did not want Howard Rice to come home and find them together. Rice was already at the table when Slocum arrived. So was Lynnanne.

"Did you have a relaxing morning, John?" Rice asked solicitously.

"Sure did, Howard." He helped himself to large portions of the light meal that had been laid out.

"Lynnanne?" Rice asked.

The girl smiled. Somehow in the past hour she had managed to repair her appearance so that once again she looked sweet and quite virginal. "I had a *very* nice morning, Daddy. You will be happy to know that Mr. Slocum is a thoroughly satisfying lover."

Slocum almost choked on a mouthful of biscuit and gravy.

Rice had been watching him. The elderly mine owner threw his head back now and roared with laughter. "Catch something in your craw, John?" he asked innocently.

"I, uh . . ."

Rice chuckled.

"Was this another of your damn tests, Howard?"

The old fellow nodded. "You acted the complete gentleman when you thought Lynnanne was my daughter," he said, "and I approve of that. But a man who won't tap an attractive lady of the evening . . . well, the man's either a candidate for sainthood—which I don't believe you are, John—or he's pretending about things."

Slocum shook his head. "Has anybody ever told you, Howard, that you're a devious old bastard?"

Rice laughed. "Of course, my friend. However else could a simple-minded old prospector come up with the capital to develop and operate a vein once he found it?"

Slocum already owed Howard Rice. More than that, though, he was beginning to like the old bastard. But Lynnanne . . . Slocum was beginning to think she had earned that spanking he had threatened her with earlier. A spanking or some other suitable form of punishment.

"Now that all the tests of character are out of the way," Rice said, "how would you feel about a trip up to the mine this afternoon, John?"

"I feel up to it," Slocum said. He was still sore—his ribs would be aching for weeks to come—but, all in all, he felt better than he had any right to expect. And confinement inside four walls was not his idea of a good time.

"Good. I think it's time you have a look around, then. You've already met Burl James. Now I want you to see the operation and meet some of the other people."

After lunch Rice had a pair of saddled horses brought around for the short climb up to the Beulah Four.

"The name Beulah comes from what I called the first burro I ever bought when I went to prospecting these mountains. And the best. She brought me luck, John. Always did. Still does, for that matter. She's retired now. I provide a home for her down lower, where the winters aren't so bad. She gets cooked bran and rolled oats twice a day and all the hay she can eat. I figure that's the least I can do for her. I've owned that burro for something like twenty years now, and Lord only knows how old she was when I got her."

"Beulah Four. Does that imply there are Beulahs One, Two, and Three as well?" Slocum asked while they rode.

Rice nodded. "Not here. They were other finds, earlier. Beulah One's in South Park. Beulah Three is up by Central City. Beulah Two was the best of them, maybe even better than this mine here. I wasn't so wise to things then, though. Brought in some 'partners' to help me develop Beulah Two. This was after I'd sold Beulah One for not much more than enough to have myself a two-month winging in Denver. And at that I probably got more than the shaft was worth. With Two, though, I brought in these partners. Figured this was a really good strike and I wanted to profit from it myself. Well, they gave me a fine education. I ought to thank them for that. They came in with lawyer-drawn partnership papers and got the operation going. Next thing I knew, they'd squeezed me out slicker than snake snot. Bought me out for ten cents a share, and at the time the company stock was worth something over eight dollars a share on the Denver market. But it was all legal. It was written down in the partnership agreement. In a way, I guess you could say they did me a favor. I learned from it. Now I don't have any partners. I got some debts from borrowing the development money, but no partners. Not ever again."

Slocum grunted. It seemed there were plenty of ways to steal from a man, some of them legal. Compared to that kind of thieving, the notion of taking a gun and taking one's chances seemed almost honest.

Rice drew rein below a rickety skeleton of timbers and connected shacks that clung to the sheer wall of the mountainside here. Over the lowest portal was a sign that said this was the Beulah Four.

"I don't understand a tenth of what I'm seeing here," Slocum admitted. "I've gone underground a few times swinging a doublejack to earn my beans when there wasn't anything else available, but I can't pretend to know anything about mining."

"It's simple enough," Rice said. He pointed high overhead. "That topmost shed up there is where the shaft is driven. The vein here runs horizontal, thank goodness. Easier that way. When you can, you start low and mine *up*. It's easier, you see, to let the ore fall of its own weight than to drag it up from a vertical shaft, especially back here where we can't haul really big engines in. So you run your shaft in low and blow stopes up into the vein to extract the ore.

"Same deal working with the ore once you have it out of the ground. You bring it out and drop it down through the stages of processing. Sort it, separate it, crush it, float it, and amalgamate it. What you end up with is a concentrate that can be shipped out and sold to refiners. The concentrate don't look like much, kind of silver-gray and shiny, but it's mostly gold from this vein with some silver, zinc, and trash metals thrown in."

Rice pointed to a fan-shaped yellow spill of pulverized rock that started about halfway up the towering mine structure and flowed down the mountainside for nearly a quarter of a mile. "That's the tailings dump," he said, "the leftover, non-metallic ore carrier that's left after the good stuff is extracted. It's what the camp took its name from." Rice grinned. "I'd been operating in here quite a while before anybody else got onto my find and came in to take up claims around me. I'm working the major vein in the district and have a few more decent ones in reserve if this one peters out. And of course mining law says I can follow my vein no matter where she takes me, regardless of surface rights. Can't go *onto* another man's claim to dig down to my vein, but I can follow mine *under* his claim just as far as she runs. Come on.''

The old miner spryly led the way up to a small, solidly built structure adjacent to but not actually connected with the rest of the incomprehensible mine workings.

No one seemed to be paying any attention at all to them but once inside the tiny building, Slocum was confronted with several pairs of shotgun muzzles leveled at him from behind protective shields of strap iron and timber.

Rice chuckled. ''It's all right, boys.''

The muzzles lowered little more than an inch.

The stout little shack was not a building, exactly, but covered the entrance to a shaft which had been blasted into the rock of the mountainside.

The shaft entrance was narrow and was flanked on each side by shielded guard stations which had also been hacked out of solid stone. Farther in, the shaft widened into a rock-walled vault where heavy canvas sacks were piled. Two more guards sat in there. They had chairs, lamps, and a table for comfort. They also had large-bored shotguns which were being held at the ready when the visitors appeared.

Rice howdied them, and they laid the shotguns aside.

''You can see, John, that the concentrate is pretty well held here. It would take a hell of a fight to get to it. The entry tunnel curves just enough that a man who could get into the outside portal couldn't get a shot into the back room here. You can see up there where we drilled bore-holes outside so the tunnel can't be blocked to smoke them out or kill the guards from lack of air. And we keep a good supply of water and food in those kegs there in case there's a long siege. I've tried to think of everything possible.''

Slocum nodded. He looked around and pretty well approved of Rice's security here. Any vault could be taken, of course, but it would take time, effort, and noise to get into this one. The odds were that no one would make a try here because he would not only have to overcome this immediate security force but would also have to control the whole camp as well. One determined man on the trail back to the outside world would be able to foil any gains made here at the mine site. Slocum told Rice that.

''That's exactly what Burl James told me,'' Rice said.

''Good.''

''Come along, then. We'll go over to the office, and you can meet my superintendent.''

Slocum followed. He felt somewhat easier once he was away from those impassive shotgun tubes. Even though their threat had been a passive rather than an active menace, he felt better for being away from them.

The Beulah Four office, located in the lowermost shack in the vertical chain that made up the mine, was a cluttered mass of paperwork, tagged ore samples, chemical bottles, and odd-looking implements, the uses for which Slocum could not begin to understand.

Amid all of it was a burly bear of a man with grit showing gray in his pores, wearing the rough clothes of a hard-rock miner.

''John Slocum, this is Jason Ferguson. Jase is the best damn mine super *either* side of the Continental Divide. Jase, Mr. Slocum here is going to work for us for a while as a special security consultant.''

Ferguson stepped forward and gave Slocum a bone-crushing handshake. ''Howdy.''

Slocum would not have taken Ferguson for a supervisor

of any kind. The man looked like a miner, right down to the rock dust that colored his clothing. Apparently the superintendent was not the kind to do his supervising from behind a desk. In fact, the only desk in the office was so cluttered it looked like it was used for storage only; it would have been impossible to find a clear space on its surface on which to work. The super apparently spent much of his time underground with his crews.

"My pleasure," Slocum said, returning the big man's handshake squeeze for squeeze.

Ferguson applied still more pressure. When, after several moments, he could not get the lean newcomer to back down or show any discomfort, he grinned and relaxed his grip. "And mine," he said. He sounded like he meant it.

"I wanted you to talk to Jase," Rice told Slocum, "because he's the one who actually picked up the rumors about us being the target of a robbery plot."

"Tell me about it," Slocum said.

"I was taking a few days off," the superintendent said. "Went up to Telluride and was raising some hell. You ought to understand that I was a mite fuzzy in the head at the time, or I'd have done some more asking instead of just laying there listening. Anyway, I was laid up in bed with this little whore up there and was telling her how I was gonna have to leave come morning because I was about down to lint in my pockets. Well, I'd been there a couple days, bought her out for that time, and we was getting along pretty good, if you know what I mean."

Slocum nodded. He was hardly in any position to judge what anyone else should do.

"And this little gal, she got to saying how if I was broke—I guess I hadn't said anything about having a job to go back to—I could maybe pick up some big money by throwing in with this crowd she'd heard was being gath-

ered for some kind of job down around Howard's Tailings.
She did't actually say it was a robbery that was planned,
but she implied it, if you know what I mean. Talked low
and kinda in circles, not ever spelling out what she was
saying, but making it clear that it was something on the far
side o' the law.''

Slocum nodded again.

"Like I said, I'd been doing some drinking before that,
and I was still doing some. Wasn't paying that much
attention to her since my ashes were hauled pretty thor-
ough by then and my head was doing some spinning. I
remember she did say something about Beulah. At the
time I had the idea she was talking about a friend of hers
with that name. It wasn't until later that I realized she was
still on the subject of this job she'd been recommending to
me.''

"What about when you sobered up?" Slocum asked.
"Why didn't you ask her more then?"

"I tried to," the superintendent said. "I was already
back down here when I made the connection. So I sent
word to Howard what I was doing and went back up to
Telluride. Time I got there, though, the girl had pulled up
and moved off to another house someplace. Some of those
gals move right regular, I guess. Or maybe she was talking
too much to other folks, too, and got herself stuffed down
an empty shaft someplace. Whatever, she wasn't there,
and nobody I asked had ever heard of her. That's the way
it is with them places. Once a girl is gone, nobody's ever
heard her name before, even if you was there plowing her
the night before. Gone in them places means they never
existed.''

Slocum grunted. It was little enough to go on, but more
than enough to make Howard Rice understandably cautious.

"I know it wasn't anything like what you were planning,''

Rice said to Slocum, "because the talk was about recruiting people to pull the robbery. Your plan was for a lone man who wouldn't even be seen and couldn't be identified. So this has to be a separate plan against the Beulah Four. The question is, what and when?"

"That could be kinda hard to learn," Slocum said. "How long ago was this?" he asked Ferguson.

The man turned to Rice for confirmation and said, "It was, what, a couple, three weeks ago?"

"Something like that," Rice said.

"That's a shame," Slocum said.

"Why?"

"If it was more recent I could go out and make myself available. In some lines of business I ain't exactly unknown, and if I asked in on something they'd be likely to grab at the chance. But if it's been that long they're sure to have their crowd put together by now. Pity. That would have been the easy way."

"I hadn't thought about that," Rice said.

Slocum grinned. "You don't exactly have the reputation that would make it a likely chance for you. I do."

Ferguson looked a bit confused, and more than a bit uneasy.

"I would trust John with my life," Rice assured him. "I *am* trusting him with my fortune."

The superintendent hesitated for only a moment. Then he visibly relaxed. "Whatever you say, Howard."

"Come along, John. If you feel up to the climb, I'll show you where your pay will come from."

Slocum had seen the inside of a mine before, but he did not want to deny the old fellow the pleasure of showing off his dream-maker. He followed as the aging prospector scrambled easily up a steep series of ladders to the shaft opening high on the mountainside and trudged inside behind Rice.

8

After supper that evening Howard Rice and Lynnanne disappeared upstairs, and Slocum got the clear impression that he would not be seeing his host again until morning. Not that Slocum could blame him. The girl was too toothsome a morsel to be left alone.

Still, thinking about what someone else was doing was not Slocum's idea of fun, nor was sitting around in a house that might as well be empty. He told Rice's maid he would be going out for a walk and headed down the hill toward the single street of the mining camp.

Howard's Tailings was not big enough to be considered a really wide-open camp, but what it lacked in size it tried to make up in sheer vigor.

There were several stores; a fair number of large rooming houses where the mining men would sleep; half a dozen saloons, each with its share of gaming tables; and at least two red-lanterned cathouses. Probably, Slocum thought, there would be a crib area too for those who had already gone through most of their pay, but wherever that tenderloin district was tucked away, he did not see it on his short walk down from Howard Rice's log mansion.

He entered the first saloon he came to and set himself up to a whiskey and a fistful of cigars.

The first whiskey tasted pretty vile after the fine liquor

he had been drinking at Rice's house. The second one went down more smoothly.

"Hello, John. Care to join us?"

Slocum turned. The man speaking to him was the mine super, Ferguson. He was at a table with a number of other men playing cards. One of the others, Slocum saw, was the security man, Burl James. "Sure." There was a vacant chair beside Ferguson, and Slocum took it.

Ferguson made a round of introductions. All of the men but one worked in some capacity at the Beulah Four. All of them greeted him pleasantly enough except for James, who glowered and mumbled something about having already met Slocum.

"Something in your craw, James?" Slocum asked.

"Damn right there is," the big security chief said.

"Name it." Slocum's expression was calm and controlled, but there was green ice glinting in his eyes.

James shifted his gaze away from the deadly danger that lay in Slocum's look and muttered something to the others about having to check on the night guards. He folded his hand in the middle of the play and left quickly.

Ferguson sent a questioning look after James, but no one at the table said anything. After a moment the mine super said, "The game is draw poker, quarter ante, nothing wild. You can open on your nerve or anything you've got to back it up. Dollar limit for each raise. If you're interested, that is."

Slocum smiled. "Oh, I reckon I could enjoy a friendly game."

"Good, because that's the kind we play here. If you want big action sometime, that's down at the Brown Burro. This table's friendly-like, and the house takes a quarter rake-off per deal."

Slocum nodded. It was relaxation these men were seeking,

not fortunes. As long as everyone else was abiding by the same rules, he would be content with the play for its own sake.

Two hours later and ahead by slightly more than eight dollars after an enjoyable run of play, Slocum bought a round of drinks for the table and passed the deal.

"Thank you, boys," he said.

"It's early," one of the men protested.

"Yeah, but my ribs are aching me pretty bad. I think it's time to pull it in and get some rest for the night."

"Come again tomorrow, if you like. We're here most evenings."

"Thanks," Slocum said again. The atmosphere at the table, indeed in the saloon, was that of men who were out to relax after a hard day's work. There had been good spirits but no troublemakers or real rowdiness. The place and the company had given Slocum a favorable impression of the men who worked in Howard's Tailings.

He stopped at the bar for a final whiskey, lighted a cigar, and stepped out onto the street. There was no board-walk in the camp, perhaps because no mill had been established to saw lumber, but the center of the street had been corduroyed with saplings to support traffic. In order to justify that in a camp no wagons could reach, Slocum thought, the spring melt must bring fierce mud and plenty of runoff.

He paused at the side of the saloon to survey the street. Lamps burned up and down the length of it, including in the stores, to accommodate the shift workers, some of whom probably never saw the light of day and others of whom might never see the stars.

Howard's Tailings was busy indeed.

Slocum thought about stopping in at the better-looking of the whorehouses to spend his poker winnings, but after the morning with Lynnanne Duffy the need was not so acute. Nor could any common whore, even a five-dollar fancy, hope to come up with the delights of Howard Rice's pretty young mistress.

He began walking slowly back up the hill. He had not been lying to the other men at the poker table. Even wrapped tightly as they now were, his ribs hurt like hell, and that combined with the thin air at this high altitude made his progress slow.

From somewhere off to his right a lance of yellow flame licked out into the darkness.

Slocum was already throwing himself sideways and down before he heard the report of the gunshot.

The .45 Colt was in his hand and cocked and he was rolling up the slope, opposite the direction the hidden gunman should have expected.

He tried to spot the bushwhacker, but the moon had not yet risen and Slocum was no longer sure of the precise point the shot had been fired from. Besides, anyone with a lick of sense would have known to move after triggering that first round.

Slocum came to his knees and the gunman fired again.

The slug sizzled by at least two feet off its target.

Slocum's answering shot was thrown just to the right of the muzzle flash. He fired and immediately scuttled uphill again, this time inching closer as well.

He heard a low cough and then a thud as something hard struck the graveled earth. That hard sound was followed by a softer thump as something else fell. Slocum thought it sounded like first a revolver and then a body striking the ground.

Taking no chances, he went to earth and crawled in a wide circle around the place where he had last seen the gunman, both to get behind the man if indeed he had gone

down and to let Slocum catch sight of the ambusher silhou-
etted against the lights of Howard's Tailings in case the
son of a bitch was not dead yet or was simply playing
possum.

The man was down, all right. Slocum could see him
now. He cat-footed forward, his Colt held at the ready.
The body on the ground did not move.

The man's revolver lay on the ground near his head.
Slocum took the final few steps in long, quick strides and
kicked the gun well out of reach.

The would-be assassin groaned.

Slocum almost triggered another round into the downed
man, thinking he might have been lying in wait with a
hideout gun, but the man groaned louder and flopped onto
his back. Both his hands were fully occupied with the
impossible chore of trying to halt the flow of blood that
was leaking out onto the ground. The blood was coming
from a point low on his chest and just to the right of
center. At the very least the man's lung had been punctured.

Slocum holstered his Colt. He had seen enough dying
men to know that there was no longer any harm in this
one. The fellow was in a state of deep shock, and all of his
attention was on his own insides. Slocum knelt beside
him.

"Why?" he asked. He had never seen the man before.
He was sure of that. Whoever the fellow was, and whatever his reason for trying to lay the ambush, Slocum had
never seen him. He was sure the man had not even been
one of the other customers in the saloon.

The man did not answer. His eyes were unfocused, his
hands still held tightly against the hole in his chest. He
was fighting a losing battle against the loss of blood,
which now spread down to darken his jeans and puddle on
the ground at his side.

"Who are you?" Slocum asked. "Why'd you try to shoot me?"

There was no response, not so much as a flicker of the man's eyes to tell that he had heard or understood the questions.

A moment more and it was too late for questions. The man slipped into unconsciousness. His eyes rolled back and his hands dropped away from his chest. His breathing became ragged and labored, and Slocum could hear the rattle of blood filling what was left of his lungs.

"Damn," Slocum muttered.

Half a minute more and the man was dead.

By then, others were gathering at the scene. Someone had brought a lantern, and men stood around Slocum and the body in a circle, whispering among themselves and asking questions to which there were no answers. Apparently death by gunshots was not so common in Howard's Tailings as to pass as a matter of course.

"Is there some law here?" Slocum asked. This time, damn it, he was not guilty of anything but self-defense, and he was *not* going to put up with any nonsense that would lead to another damned wanted poster with his name on it.

No one responded. This time Slocum picked out one individual in particular to address and asked his question again.

The man looked nervous. "Not really," he said.

"Mr. Rice's man Burl James is as close as we can come, I reckon," another man said.

"Get him," Slocum told the fellow. When the man hesitated, Slocum added a curt "Now!" The man went, trotting off into the night.

James appeared a few minutes later. He was alone. Apparently the man Slocum had sent to fetch him had found other business more pressing than that of staring at a corpse.

Burl James made no effort to hide his dislike for Slocum, nor was he inclined to show any fear. "Did you have a reason to kill this poor son of a bitch, Slocum?" he asked. "Or don't you need one?"

"There's his gun," Slocum said, pointing. "Check it. Then ask me again."

"I seen it, Mr. James," one of the miners said. "I was over there, comin' out of the alley there. I seen this feller here shoot an' then shoot again, an' this feller shot back an' the first one dropped."

James grunted something and bent to pick up the dead man's gun. He flipped the loading gate aside and punched the shells out into his palm. The revolver had been loaded with six cartridges instead of the usual five, sure indication that immediate use and as much firepower as possible had been intended, because a so-called sixgun was normally carried with an empty chamber under the hammer for safety reasons. There were two spent shells and four live rounds in James's hand. The big man grunted again, as if he did not like finding confirmation of the miner's story of the shooting.

"Let me have your gun," James demanded.

Slocum gave him a wolfish smile that had no hint of humor or good will in it. "Sure. Any time you're man enough to take it off me."

James bristled but did not pursue it any further. Instead he changed the subject entirely. "Who is he?" he demanded.

Slocum shrugged.

Another man in the still-growing crowd spoke up. "I know him. Knew 'im, that is. His name's Mickey. Catalanos, Caladenas, something Eyetalian-sounding like that. Mickey for short."

"Does he—I mean, did he work in one of the mines?" Slocum asked.

The miner shook his head. "Mule packer. Used to be. I met him over at the Pink Garter. He was kinda coming off a drunk. Said he'd been drinking and lost his mule string an' didn't know what he'd do next." The man frowned. "He said he had a wife an' some kids on the outside someplace an' he didn't know how he was going to go home broke an' face them like that."

"That's it then," Burl James said.

"What is?" Slocum asked.

"Obvious," James said. "He was broke and tried to get a stake by robbery. He just picked the wrong fellow to gun down. Bad luck all the way around, eh?"

Slocum opened his mouth to disagree, but clamped his jaws shut again before he spoke.

Whoever this down-and-out Mickey had been, he was not planning to roll the first person to come along. With a knife or a club as the weapon, Slocum might have accepted that. But not with a revolver, Gunshots draw attention. Even if Mickey had been successful in his ambush there would have been no time for him to run out into the relatively well lighted area where Slocum had been walking and pick his victim clean in time to make a getaway. No, Slocum thought, robbery was not what Italian Mickey had had in mind here.

He did not disagree with Burl James's assessment out loud. But he did not accept it either.

James began giving orders to several of the men who were gathered. So-and-so were to take the body to thus-and-such place. Somebody else was to be told to bury him. So-and-so was to cut a headstone or carve one. The Beulah Four would pay the bill for the burying.

The men James had designated picked up Mickey's

lifeless form and carried it away. The rest of the crowd
began to move off. Soon only Slocum and Burl James
remained.

Slocum stood slouching in the path, seemingly casual,
but intent on watching James. When they were alone he
asked, "Do you still want my gun?"

James looked at him. He seemed to be giving serious
consideration to what amounted to a challenge. After a
moment the tension went out of the big man's shoulders.
"No. Not right now, mister." He grinned, and Slocum did
not like what he saw in Burl James's face. "Another time,
Slocum. Another place."

"Any time, any place," Slocum assured him.

James turned away and walked back toward the saloons.
Slocum waited until James was out of sight before he
turned and resumed his walk back up the hill toward
Howard Rice's mansion.

9

"Mr. Slocum?"

"Yes, Miss, uh . . ."

The maid gave him a dimpled smile and helped him out. "Catherine, sir."

"Sorry. What was it you wanted, Catherine?"

"Mr. Rice and Miss Duffy have retired for the evening, sir, but Mr. Rice wanted you to know that your things have been brought in. He had them taken up to your room, sir. And he left word that I should assist you if you would like a bath before you change. If you like, sir, I can also have those clothes laundered for you now."

"That sounds fine, Catherine. Thanks."

"Yes, sir." She gave him another smile and a brief hint of a curtsy, then efficiently whisked away to begin hauling his bath water upstairs.

Slocum helped himself to some of Howard Rice's whiskey and climbed the stairs with a slow, weary step. He had not been aware of the pain still in his ribs when he was talking back to the would-be bushwhacker named Mickey, but now he ached practically from his neck downward.

Catherine had a wooden tub half full of warm water waiting in his bedroom. The water looked inviting.

"You look tired, sir."

"I am," he told her.

The maid began to help him out of his clothing. He saw with some relief that his saddlebags and bedroll were by the foot of the bed. He was anxious to get into a shirt that did not have the odor of an elderly mule. Then it occurred to him what Catherine was doing. He stopped her hands just short of his belt buckle.

"What are you doing?"

"I was told to assist you, sir. And I do scrub a back rather well."

Slocum suspected that he really ought to feel embarrassed. What he felt was horny. It was like that sometimes after a fight, and he had been more than half hoping that Howard would already have dismissed Lynnanne for the evening. Still, this Catherine was downright pretty, too. Howard had mighty fine taste when it came to women, it seemed.

"Is that all you do well?" he asked.

Her answer was an impish smile.

He let her help him out of the rest of his clothes and accepted her hand to steady him as he crawled into the tub and settled deep in the soothing water. He sighed.

Catherine knelt on the rug beside the tub and, as promised, proved to be an excellent back washer. She took up another handful of the soft soap and began to spread it over his chest.

"If you don't stop pretty soon," he said, "I think we're fixing to have a problem here."

Catherine laughed. "If *that* is what you're talking about, the problem has already risen." She pointed down toward the bath water in front of Slocum's waist. There, peeking through a film of soap, was a red, rock-hard bulb.

"Kind of obvious, huh?"

"Lean back a little."

"Why?"

"I'm supposed to help you get clean, aren't I?"

Slocum leaned back.

The pretty maid ran her fingertips over him. Her hand disappeared under the surface of the water to envelop his shaft in a gentle grip. She began rubbing him as if she was washing him, but judging from the expression on her face he did not think she had cleanliness in mind at the moment.

"If you keep that up," Slocum told her, "you're apt to get splashed with something that ain't soap and ain't water, and then we'll both need to get clean again."

Catherine giggled. "It really would not do, sir, for you to get my uniform all spotted and sticky, would it?"

"I agree," Slocum said, "that would be terribly unfair of me when you're trying to be helpful."

"But what do you think we could do to avoid that?"

"Mmmm, one way would be for you to take the uniform off. Remove it from the danger, so to speak."

She pretended deep thought while she continued to stroke him with her hand. "That would be one possibility, yes."

"Can you think of a better one?"

"Perhaps not a *better* one, but an *additional* precaution."

"And what might that be?" Slocum asked.

"Well, sir, we could relieve some of the pressure that threatens to cause the problem. Deposit the sticky substance elsewhere."

"Do you think that would help?"

"We could certainly give it a try, sir."

"I reckon I'm willing to try if you are," Slocum said. "Just to keep from getting your uniform mussed, of course."

"Of course, sir." Catherine released her hold on him and stood. She removed her apron and slipped out of her rather severe uniform dress. She was not wearing anything under the dress.

She was short and her figure was not as lush as Lynnanne's, but she had a trim, nicely rounded form.

Slocum chuckled when he saw that, like Rice's mistress, Rice's maid was shaved completely bald where her pubic hair should have been. Apparently Lynnanne Duffy was not the only one who bedded the master of the house and was required to meet the old gentleman's odd tastes.

Catherine kicked off her shoes and spun around for Slocum to admire. "Satisfactory, sir?" she asked.

"Quite," he assured her.

He stood, water streaming down from his lean body, his erection poking abruptly out from his loins and bobbing slightly with every heartbeat.

"Oh, my," Catherine said. "That *is* lovely, sir."

"Satisfactory?" he asked.

"Quite." She laughed and picked up a towel to dry him with.

Slocum let the girl attend to him. Then he led her over to the broad, soft bed. The previous night he had occupied that bed in extreme discomfort after Lynnanne's visit. Tonight he did not think he was going to have that same problem.

He lay down and Catherine molded herself against him. Her body was warm and soft against his cool, damp flesh.

"I missed a spot when I was drying you," Catherine said. She raised herself on one elbow until she was poised over him and bent her head to begin licking a few lingering drops of water from his chest.

"You missed another spot," he told her.

"Really? Where? Never mind. I see." With a delighted laugh her head moved lower, and her tongue began to play along the hard, throbbing shaft of his cock.

"I think you found it," Slocum said.

"I think I did indeed, sir."

Her head dipped lower, and she licked his balls.

"I think you missed that spot rather badly," Slocum said.

"I do believe I did, sir. But perhaps I can do better this way."

She mouthed his scrotum and pulled one over-full nut into her mouth, sucking on it gently and rolling her tongue over it.

"Much better," Slocum croaked.

Catherine released him and raised her head to give him a smile. "Can you think of anyplace else I might have missed, sir?"

"One, maybe?"

"Here?" She leaned forward and flicked the head of his cock with her tongue. The thing bounced high with an involuntary reaction, and Catherine laughed. She did it again and got the same reaction from him.

"That must be the spot," Slocum said.

"I really must clean it properly," Catherine said in mock seriousness.

She took him into her mouth, the warmth of her engulfing and tantalizing him. She held him there loosely, applying no suction at all now while the warmth of her seeped into his flesh. Then, softly at first, she began to suck on him.

Slocum moaned. "You better quit that or you're fixing to have a mouthful," he said.

Her response was to suck on him harder. Her fingertips found his balls and stroked him gently there. She must have been able to feel his mounting excitement, because she began to bob her head up and down with increasing speed, never losing him and continuing to apply the warm, eager suction.

Slocum stiffened and shuddered as he exploded into her. He came in a series of hot spurts that seemed to go on and on, one after another, and Catherine rode with him through it all, never losing the grip of her lips and mouth until he thought sure she was in danger of drowning.

Even when he was completely done she stayed with him, and after little more than a minute he began to throb toward complete readiness again.

Catherine returned to her sucking and stroking, seeming to expect that he would want her to stay there and bring him off the second time that way also, but Slocum pulled her away and rolled her onto her back on the soft, comfortable bed at his side.

"Is that the only way you like it?" he asked.

She smiled and shook her head. "Habit," she said.

"Oh."

"I really would like to feel that big thing of yours inside me, sir."

"Good. Because that's exactly what I intend to do with it." He rolled on top of her, and Catherine opened herself to him.

Lynnanne had been tight. The maid Catherine was like trying to wedge it into a keyhole. He had to push so hard to enter her that, in spite of her obvious level of experience in other areas, he actually began to wonder if she might be still a virgin down there. If she had not been so wet and ready to receive him he probably could not have gotten into her at all, and as it was it took the cooperative effort of them both before he finally was able to squeeze and squirm full depth inside her.

Catherine's eyes widened, and she sighed with sheer contentment as he filled her.

"Are you all right?" he asked.

She nodded happily. "For a minute there," she said, "I thought it was going to reach my throat from the wrong direction, but it's fine now. Just fine.'' She wrapped her arms around him and clung to him.

He waited patiently until he felt the tension leave her. Her thighs, which had been clamped hard against him, relaxed and fell comfortably open to him. Only then did he begin to stroke in and out.

He moved slowly at first, giving her time to adjust to the penetration. He could feel her breath quicken, coming in short, panting gasps against his chest. Only then did he allow himself to stroke hard and fast into her receptive body. Only then did he give himself free rein to root and plunge until he again exploded, this time deep within her.

He was distantly aware of Catherine's matching climax. She squealed out loud, trying in vain to muffle the sound against his chest, and clutched him with a fierce strength. Her arms and legs locked in a vise grip around him, and he could feel a hard, fluttery series of contractions from the shaven lips of her sex.

''Lucky,'' he said.

''What?'' she asked in a small, weak voice.

''I said that was lucky. I don't think we got a drop of it on your uniform.''

Catherine sighed and held him tightly. ''Let's be *real* sure we don't, okay?''

''I always try to oblige,'' he assured her.

She began to kiss the hard slabs of muscle on his chest, the only part of him she could reach at that moment. Mighty appreciative, Slocum thought. And *so* concerned about not getting her uniform soiled.

Howard Rice ladled some gravy onto a biscuit and reached for the salt. ''I see you got your things,'' he said.

''I did. Thank you for going to the trouble.''

''No trouble at all. Your saddle and bridle are out in the

shed. The scabbard is on the saddle, I'm told, but my man couldn't find your rifle, if you had one."

"I had one," Slocum said.

"It must have fallen into the creek."

Slocum shrugged. Rifles could be replaced. He had been damned lucky to come out of the accident alive.

"Did Catherine take care of you all right last night?" Rice asked.

"Fine," Slocum assured him.

"Good." Rice looked up and gave him a wink.

Damm it, Slocum thought, *a man likes to have some privacy.* Rice did not seem to share that opinion.

"I'll be working in the office today," Rice said. "And I have an early appointment with a chemicals salesman. Come along up to the workings whenever you feel up to it. I'll leave word with Burl to go over the shipment schedule with you. You might get some ideas from that."

"All right."

"If there is anything else you need, anything at all, ask Catherine. She has been instructed to make sure you are completely comfortable while you are here, John."

"Thanks." Slocum had mixed feelings about that, though. The maid was a delightful partner for a romp, as he had cause to know, but having Rice's approval for it—and instructions to the girl—gave the whole thing the flavor of pandering. Slocum neither wanted nor needed that. He wondered if his host would be offended if he mentioned it, then decided to let it pass for the time being.

Rice finished his breakfast in a hurry and left for the office. Slocum enjoyed a more leisurely meal and went back upstairs to shave before he got about the business Howard Rice was depending on him for.

10

The climb up to the Beulah Four was neither that far nor that steep, but Slocum took his time about it. He was still more sore than he would have cared to admit, and the exertions of the night before had done nothing to make him feel any better. He was about to become annoyed with himself, though. For as long as he could remember he had been blessed with remarkable health, and on those occasions when he had received an injury, including assorted knife and bullet wounds, he had always been quick to heal. The continued soreness in his ribs was bothersome for more than the actual aches and pains. It was a reminder of the fact that he no longer had the vitality of a brash kid in his twenties.

He chose to walk instead of asking Catherine for a saddle horse because he thought the exercise might do him good, help limber up muscles that a man seldom used in this wide, high country where a horse was as necessary as a gun.

And, he admitted to himself, he chose to walk because the morning air was just so damned invigorating. There was a crisp, hard bite to the air at this altitude that a lowlander could never hope to experience. It was not a matter of cold, exactly, although the air was certainly still chill several hours after the sun rose above the rim of the surrounding mountains. It was something more than that, something Slocum took pleasure in experiencing even if he did not know its cause.

It felt good too to have on a clean shirt and drawers and his ragged but clean pair of spare jeans. The clothes he had been wearing when the Palouse fell had begun to feel like they were sticking to his skin, and it had been a pleasure to turn them over to Catherine for washing.

He climbed the last relatively steep section of the short trail and paused for a breather. His ribs were bothering him some, and he used the excuse of a look down over the camp of Howard's Tailings to justify his stop as not exactly a rest but an opportunity to look over the camp from a different angle.

The path here curved around a point of slick vertical rock that reminded him all too much of the trail he had so recently fallen from.

He looked over the camp for a moment. From here he was able to see the line of cribs clinging to the hillside behind the single street of the camp which he had not spotted the night before when he went into town. Downhill from the street the terrain was not so steep. There he could see a large number of shacks and tiny cabins built against the hillside with paths leading up to the business district. There was also one larger building set well away from the other commercial structures. That one had a cross set into the earth in front of it.

If Howard's Tailings had a church, Slocum thought, there would probably be plans for a school next. And then, inevitably, there would be some sort of formal government organized, and someone was sure to raise the question of taxes. Not that Slocum disapproved. That was just the way things went. He recognized the fact of it without passing judgement.

He turned and started up the trail again, then paused to pull out a cigar and light it.

A few feet ahead of him he saw a thin trickle of gravel fall to the level of the path. The light gravel struck the rock with an almost musical tinkle and bounced away down the hillside.

Slocum looked up. Far overhead a huge boulder teetered. It must have been that massive rock coming loose that dislodged the gravel.

The boulder tilted forward and began to tumble end over end with a slow, almost majestic progression of speed and mass.

Slocum grunted and took a few steps backward.

The boulder crashed onto the path not more than a dozen feet in front of him. Flying splinters of shattered stone pelted the trail and the rock wall. Even through the solid rock of the path Slocum could feel the impact of the awesome weight when the boulder hit. The sound was oddly small and dull.

The great chunk of stone struck and spun and rolled off the trail to bound its way down toward Howard's Tailings, eventually coming to rest against the stump of a long-dead tree. The tree stump split apart but held its place, and no harm was done. The boulder might lie there for another hundred years before gravity overcame the resistance of the slowly rotting stump. Or the next rainfall might send it tumbling again.

The likelihood, though, of any damage resulting the next time the boulder fell was slight. The odds on being hit by a falling rock were only slightly greater than those of being struck by lightning: damned slim.

Slocum thought about that and looked from where the boulder had come to rest back up to where it had fallen from.

Damned unlikely that anyone would be hurt.

Yet had he not stopped to light that cigar, it was very possible he might have been walking on that exact bit of path where the great rock had fallen, at exactly the moment it struck.

It was, in fact, very likely that he would have been.

Slocum jammed the cigar between his teeth and chewed on the wet end of it reflectively for a moment.

What were the odds, he wondered, that would have put him just there, just then? Or the odds that he would decide after already starting forward to stop and pull out a smoke?

He looked up again, craning his neck and examining the wall of rock carefully, but he could see nothing of interest up there.

A few days before, he remembered quite clearly, he had been lying hurt and in need of help just a matter of feet below the trail in to Howard's Tailings. He had not been able to see the men passing overhead until they heard him and leaned out to see where he was.

He was no more likely to see what was above him now than he could then.

Interesting, he thought. *Almighty interesting.*

There was a question that was beginning to nag at him now.

The easy way to resolve that question was to simply forget about it and go on to the Beulah Four.

But John Slocum had not lived as long as he already had by doing things the easy way.

He ran a hand over his ribs and told the damn things that they were not going to stop him from answering the question that was in his mind.

His decision made now, he began moving back and forth along the path, looking for a way to climb up to the level where that boulder had fallen from.

*   *   *

He was out of breath and had had to stop several times to rest, but he had gotten there. He climbed the last few feet by pulling himself hand over hand up a series of slim fingerholds, but he made it.

There was a broad ledge here covered with a thin layer of pea gravel and loose soil. A few trees grew here, and some patches of grass. At the back of the ledge there was some moss or possibly lichen clinging to the bare rock. As Slocum expected, there was no one in sight.

He seated himself on a boulder that was a twin to the one which had fallen and lighted another cigar. Probably his lungs did not need the rasping assault of the smoke at that moment, but he wanted the cigar, and to hell with his lungs. It took him several minutes to get his breathing back under control, and he reminded himself that the altitude would have as much to do with that as the exertion.

When he felt up to it he began inching along the rim of the ledge, intent on examining the ground there.

It was easy enough to spot the place where the boulder had fallen from.

Slocum was a fair hand as a tracker and would have had no trouble anyway in locating an empty pocket that so recently held a heavy boulder.

But a blind half-wit could have spotted this.

There was a four-foot-long steel prybar lying on the ground there and a number of chalk-white scratch marks on the rock at the rim of the ledge.

Interesting, Slocum thought. *Almighty interesting.*

That boulder would have crushed him like an ant under a boot heel, and no one would have questioned the "accident." No one at all. A freak chance? Sure. But old John Slocum would have been too dead to ask any questions, and no one else was likely to ask them for him.

Shee-it, Slocum thought.

They, or he, would have gotten away with it. Gotten away with it clean.

Just plain bad luck would have been the way it was taken, and that would have been the end of John Slocum.

Except that he stopped to light a cigar.

Slocum took another look around the wide ledge, and this time there was a glint of ice and steel in his eyes, and his lips were drawn back into a thin smile that held no humor, only more of that cold fire that was in his eyes.

If you want to dance, boys, he silently told the unknown hand or hands that had been on the end of that prybar, *come on out and we'll see who pays the fiddler.*

Slocum ached for some son of a bitch to come out and face him. That ache was infinitely worse than anything he could have felt in his sore ribs. In fact, he was no longer conscious of his ribs in the slightest.

He just wanted someone to face and to fight. Anyone. Any damn number of anyones. The whole camp could come at him right now, and he would pile into them one at a time or all together, any way they wanted it. Just so he could fight back.

Bastards! Ambushing, bushwhacking, murdering pricks, he seethed.

He drew back his foot and gave the discarded prybar a kick that sent it spinning out into space and down toward the trail to the Beulah Four.

But there was no one here to fight.

Slocum calmed down and got himself back under control.

Ambushing, bushwhacking, murdering pricks? It was quite a coincidence, he realized, that last night someone tried to shoot him out of the darkness and today someone tried to plant a boulder on top of his hat.

Perhaps too much of a coincidence. Perhaps one whole hell of a lot too much to be coincidence.

Slocum wished now that his bullet had not finished the down-and-out man called Mickey. He had been skeptical at the time about Mickey's intention being robbery. Now he was convinced that it had been something more.

But Mickey was dead now. He damn sure was not the one who had wielded the prybar today.

So someone else, possibly the same one who hired Mickey, was wanting John Slocum dead.

There were several possibilities about why that might be so. Someone could well have seen some of those wanted posters Slocum so despised. Yet none of the rewards were so large that a man was likely to hire his killing done. Possible, but not really likely that that was the reason.

His employment by Howard Rice, then. *That* was more likely.

If someone was intending to make a big score off Howard Rice and the Beulah Four, it was very likely that he or they would want Slocum dead.

Apparently the man who was planning the job had figured out how to get around Burl James and his guards. But the man did not believe he could necessarily get around Slocum's peculiar expertise with robbery plans.

Slocum sneered at the empty, forbidding mountains that surrounded him, but his thoughts were directed toward the unseen man or men who were so obviously afraid of what he might discover here.

All right, you bastards, he told them. *Come for me. Any time, any way. Come for me, and I'll put you down, kicking and hollering, and I'll give you all the mercy of a boulder falling off a high, high ledge. Come for me now.*

11

"Damn it, John, there is no reason why you should go out this evening," Rice said hotly. They were seated in the old man's study having a whiskey after supper. "If it's company you want, Catherine is here. She tells me she would be delighted to ease your loneliness again. If it's conversation, hell, man, I'll sit up late and talk your ears sore. That is one of the good things about getting older, you know—plenty of stories to tell. Either way, we can provide for your needs right here in this house. And here there is no one trying to kill you. At least here you are safe."

Slocum drained his glass and set it aside on the low table. "It isn't that, Howard, although I thank you for being worried about me. I get restless sometimes, and I like to get around and hear things." He grinned. "Besides, I feel lucky tonight. I want to sit in on a card game again."

"My people won't be at the usual game tonight, John. Ferguson won't be there to play with. Neither will Burl."

"Why is that, Howard?"

The old man gave Slocum a sly grin. "Because the ante just went up on one of those shipments you'll be guarding."

"What happened?"

"Do you know what a vug is, John?"

Slocum shook his head. He thought he might have heard

the word before, but if so its meaning had escaped him since then.

"A vug is a pocket, usually an air pocket or empty bubble inside the rock. Sometimes—not often, but sometimes when a vug is formed—mineral-bearing fluid seeps into the pocket and leaves its deposits of minerals behind when it leaks out again. A vug can then become a pocket of virtually pure gold." Rice's grin grew wider and he insisted on pouring another drink for each of them.

"The afternoon powder shot in Number Three drift broke into a vug today. The chamber is two feet around and about a foot and a half deep, and it was nearly filled with raw gold, John. Not concentrate, mind. This material won't even have to go through the crusher. It can be sold just as it is. Of course, we don't have the test results on the purity, but that hardly matters. I can tell you just from working with a piece of it that the material is virtually pure. It's as malleable as jeweler's gold just as it comes from the rock."

Slocum whistled. A chunk of raw gold like that would be worth . . . he could not begin to calculate the amount. It would be a pretty penny; he was certain of that. So, judging by the old man's excitement, was Howard Rice.

"Congratulations, Howard."

"The contents of that vug, John, could go a long way toward eliminating the last of my debt on the Beulah Four. It could wipe out my last obligations from the capital I had to borrow to start the mine and put me over the top. After this I might not have to worry about threats to my cash flow the way I do now. It could mean a lot to me, John, and to every miner and gang boss I employ here."

"I'm glad for you, Howard. Genuinely glad. But that is all the more reason why I should be out and around tonight. I might hear something. Or some son of a bitch might make another try for me. If anybody does, with luck, I might be able to take him and ask the man a few questions. We need to know what these people are so afraid of, Howard, and who they are. Then we can be certain to protect your shipments and get them out to the refinery.''

''Let me do one thing then, John,'' Rice said. ''Let me assign one of my security men as a bodyguard for you. Or a pair of them. Yes, that might be better. I can have some of my people watch over you.''

John Slocum threw his head back and laughed loud and long. A bodyguard for the he-coon of the empty country? The very idea of it brought tears of laughter to his often cold eyes.

''You can sit in on this game, neighbor,'' the man invited. Slocum had been wandering among the tables for several minutes now. Apparently this gambler had spotted him as a mark.

Slocum smiled at the man and took the offered chair.

The gambler who seemed to be running the table was a tall, slender dude with soft hands and hard eyes. His clothing was an attempt to make him fit in with the roughly dressed miners, but his physique and quick, dexterous fingers did not fit in with that intended image.

''Workin' man?'' the gambler asked.

''Oh, you could say I'm on the drift right now,'' Slocum told him. ''I came up from the south with a little stake in my pocket and thought I'd take a look around this part of the country. I might take a job when that runs out, or I might get lucky here tonight and not have to work for a spell longer. We'll see how it goes.''

The gambler's eyes tightened slightly when Slocum mentioned having a stake in his pocket. The man nodded with a display of feigned pleasure and reached out to the side to stroke the flank of a girl who was hanging over him. "For luck," he explained.

"Sure," Slocum said.

There were three other men at the table, all dressed as miners, although one of them had suspiciously clean hands. Slocum marked him as a shill and card snitch for the head of the team. The man would be there to keep the betting going when the gambler could not and to exchange winning cards from his hand for losers out of the dealer's hand whenever necessary.

It was not a bad system for suckers. Slocum had been down this pike a few times too many to fall for their game. But they might not know that.

There was a good chance that the girl was in on it too, Slocum saw. She was not dressed for bar work and whoring, although she looked capable of handling that when their pockets were running light.

She was a slat-thin girl, fairly tall, with a pinched, pouty face some men might think fairly pretty. Her whole attention was on her gambler rather than the free-spending drinkers milling past, which strengthened Slocum's suspicion that she might be part of the play.

A girl like that, once she knew the proper signals, could be sent on little errands for drinks or cigars and come back with an eyefull to report about the other players hands. A touch of the cheek or a faintly transmitted set of prearranged taps on the back of the gambler's neck, and the man would know the contents of every hand the girl had seen in her travels.

A setup like that could be damned convenient, Slocum acknowledged. And interesting to play against.

"We have a friendly game here, mister," the gambler

said. "No limits, nothing wild, dealer's choice between draw and stud. My name is Hank Farloe. Yours?"

"John," Slocum said.

"It's our pleasure, John. The fellow to your left there is Pete, then Henry, and Wiley on my right. The lady here is Pearl." He smiled. "She's my luck, you see." He ran his hand down her thigh again, and Pearl smiled, exposing a small gap in her front teeth. Slocum suspected the man called Wiley of being a partner in Hank Farloe's game.

Farloe picked up the deck of cards and announced the game as draw poker. He shuffled and dealt rather awkwardly. That was an old, old trick, and one Slocum thought would have been pitched out of any professional's play a long time ago. It was supposed to prove that the man could not mechanic the deck because he did not handle it well. What it proved to Slocum instead was that Hank Farloe was out of his league whenever he was playing with anybody but a rube fresh from the farm.

The hand Slocum was given—not dealt, he was sure, but deliberately given—held a four, five, seven, eight, and jack in mixed suits.

It was all Slocum could do to keep from smiling at how obvious Farloe was being. The man wanted to find out if he would draw to an inside straight.

Always happy to oblige, Slocum chucked the jack and held onto the rest. Lo and behold—oh, how amazed he was!—he was "lucky" enough to pull the missing six on the draw.

As soon as the betting began, it became obvious why Farloe wanted a new hand in the game. Pete and Henry apparently were close to being tapped out. Their bets were small and hesitant, and they played like men who were just trying to hang on until their luck changed. Apparently neither of them realized that luck had nothing to do with Hank Farloe's play.

The pot was small, and Slocum was allowed to win it. He was just practically overwhelmed by the joy of it all.

Under other circumstances, just to annoy the man, he might have collected that pot, thanked them all, and walked away. In fact, when a man was on his uppers, that could be a pretty handy way to get enough of a stake for a meal and a bed until something better showed up.

But this evening he felt like playing some more. And he saw no reason in the world why Hank Farloe's little game should be a deterent to his having some fun. So he pitched in his ante for the next deal and went on about the business of letting Mr. Farloe try and take his fleece.

Farloe obviously had already dismissed the other two players, because the competition was completely between the gambler and Slocum. Wiley was allowed an occasional pot also, just to keep things from seeming too completely obvious, but neither Pete nor Henry was in on the play. Farloe was giving them such poor cards now that it was clear he was only trying to milk them for a last few coins.

Pete dropped out three hands later, and Farloe gave Henry a small winner just to keep the table reasonably full.

In the meantime, Slocum's stake was slowly dwindling.

Farloe had a pretty fair touch about that, Slocum acknowledged. The man was not trying to take it all in one kill, but was content to nibble at it a bit at a time.

With the deal passing around the table, either Farloe or his man Wiley had the cards half of the time, so he had more than enough opportunity to work his mechanical skills on the deck.

When Wiley dealt, Pearl usually was busy bringing drinks—and telegraphing the contents of hands—so it was clear that Wiley was not the mechanic Farloe was.

The poor slob tried a second deal once, and he did it so badly that Slocum felt sorry for him. With even a halfway efficient mechanic handling the deck the only way to detect a false deal should be through the play and not the hands. Wiley was plainly out of his league even attempting the tricks of his dangerous trade, and Slocum probably would have been doing Farloe a favor if he shot Wiley.

But he was having more fun this way.

Henry was forced out of the game on his own deal. Pearl must have signaled that Henry had an unusually good hand, because for the first time since Slocum sat in, Farloe and Wiley made a switch. It was not particularly well done. Wiley yawned, and his hand disappeared behind Pearl's back. Then Farloe gave the girl another stroke for "luck," and Wiley yawned again. Each of them had had a hand out of sight behind the girl for a moment, and Slocum was sure some cards had been exchanged. He threw in three tens and folded, waiting to see what happened to the unsuspecting Henry.

The poor man bet the last cent in his pocket, and Farloe made a show of reluctantly covering it. He could legitimately have overcalled, but he did not. When the hands were shown, Henry had a full house, but Farloe won the pot with four treys. Slocum wondered how many of those had come out of Wiley's hand.

Henry, busted until his next payday, groaned his way out into the night.

Taking the man had been bad enough, Slocum thought, but Farloe did not even exhibit the common courtesy of standing the man to drinks at the bar when he was forced away from the table.

Farloe probably had no idea why the man called John was giving him a somewhat wolfish grin across the felt-covered table.

"It's down to the three of us now, boys," Farloe said as he raked his money into a pile in front of him. "What say we speed this along and run the ante up?"

"I'm willin'," Wiley said.

"Oh, I reckon I can go along with that," Slocum allowed.

It was Slocum's deal. He shuffled quickly, building a bottom stack that he thought was damn well appropriate in honor of the now-departed Henry. He put the four treys on the bottom with four hearts and a spade below them.

Wiley cut, and Slocum deftly returned the deck to its original shape as he picked up the cards and began to deal.

Wiley was given whatever legitimately came off the top of the deck. Farloe received the near flush. Slocum gave himself a fair deal that turned out to be three tens, a queen and a king. He promptly held the king and threw the rest in.

Wiley drew three cards and, as expected, Farloe took one.

Slocum dealt straight to Wiley and gave Farloe a fifth heart to make his flush. He bottom-dealt the four threes to himself, knowing damn good and well that Farloe would know but would not dare call the raw deal.

Wiley must have received a signal from Farloe, because he started the betting and started it big, with Farloe following and raising.

"I'll tell you what, boys," Slocum said, "I'm getting a little tired and a little horny and I wanta get out of here. Let's push it on this hand and see where she falls."

Farloe brightened considerably with that flush in his hand, and Wiley was allowed to drop out. The gambler counted his money and pushed the pile into the center of the table. "I'll go along with that, John, and raise you ninety-four dollars."

"I can see your raise, Hank, and up you, let's see here," Slocum pulled a palmful of double eagles from his pocket and clanked them onto the table, "say a hundred."

"I don't have that much with me, John," Farloe said.

"Then I reckon the pot's mine," Slocum said. He reached for it.

"I could loan you a few dollars," Wiley said, earning him a warning glare from his partner. Wiley shut up.

Still, Farloe was sure he could beat Slocum's hand, which he still believed was a straight deal and probably a last hand bluff, with this John trying to buy the hand before he left.

"I can cover you, John."

"Fine. Put it on the table."

"Back in my room . . ."

"On the table, Hank, or we say good night," Slocum said coldly.

The gambler thought for a moment. "I could put Pearl up for my shortage."

Slocum looked her over critically. "Two dollars' worth?"

The girl blanched but did not say anything.

"I'm not talking use, John, but ownership. Ol' Pearl there, she can keep you in grub when you aren't working." He gave Slocum a wink. "Put Pearl on the line and she could make a rich man of you."

"Sure." Slocum looked at the girl again. "All right. The bet's covered." He laid down his hand, exposing the same four treys Farloe had just used to cheat Henry out of the last of his money.

Farloe gave him an odd look. He looked even paler than usual.

"I've enjoyed watching you play," Slocum said, "but

you could use a little more practice in front of a mirror. It ain't necessarily healthy for you to count on your friends here to tell you how you're doing, 'cause they don't know what to look for any more than you do, tinhorn.''

Color rushed to Farloe's face, and with a shake of his arm a dark, deadly little derringer appeared in his fist.

Poor dumb Wiley turned out to be loyal to his boss. Too loyal for his own health. He went for his gun too, grabbing for his armpit.

Slocum palmed his Colt and put both of them out of their misery with a thunder roll of rapid pistol fire at tabletop range. Farloe and Wiley were on the floor with their blood staining the sawdust before the ringing had died out of the other patrons' ears.

Calmly Slocum reached across the table and raked the pot in. He left Wiley's pile untouched.

''You there,'' he said to the bartender, who was holding a bung-starter that he now had no intention of using. ''Do you know a couple of men named Henry and Pete who were just cleaned out at this table?''

The bartender nodded.

''That pile over there belongs to them. Split it between them. They were cheated. If that doesn't go far enough to cover their losses, tell them to look me up.''

''Yes, sir.''

Slocum was out the door and halfway up the hill to Howard Rice's mansion before he realized that Pearl was doggedly tagging behind him.

''Go home, girl,'' he said.

''Don't have one.''

''Find one.''

She started to cry. ''I never been on my own, mister. I can't go off by my own self. I *can't*. You got to take care of me now, mister. You took the bet, didn' you? Now you gotta take care of me. You *got* to." She was crying harder and harder.

Slocum stood in the dark street cursing. He did not know *what* the hell to do now that he seemed to have won his own private, personal slave.

12

"Damn it, Pearl, I . . . It is Pearl, isn't it?"

She nodded unhappily.

"The thing is, Pearl, I can't take you back to the house I've been staying in." Hauling a drab, mousy little slattern like Pearl into Howard Rice's home was hardly proper conduct for a guest. Especially since the slattern seemed intent on blubbering and bawling into the night.

"I ain't never been alone, mister, not never in my whole life," Pearl wailed. "You *got* to take care of me." Her lips peeled back from a mouthful of uneven teeth into what must have been intended as a seductive smile. "I'll be real good to you, mister, honest I will. I turned tricks for Hank lots of times when we was broke. You'll like me, I swear you will. Just don't leave me alone now. You're 'sponsible for me now, mister. You can't leave me. Jus' stick with me an' I'll prove to you how fine I can be for you." She clutched at his elbow with desperate strength.

The damned girl was serious. Slocum had no doubt about that at all. She was petrified by the idea of being left to fend for herself.

"Look," Slocum said apologetically, "I just don't have a place . . ."

"We can go t' the cabin."

"What cabin?"

"Hank an' Wiley an' me, we had us a cabin down the hill there. Kinda a out of the way place where nobody'd have to see that Wiley was with us, see. It's rented. All paid for an' everything. Hank told me that. It's paid up for near another month. We could go there. But, mister, you just gotta stay with me tonight. I swear I'd be so scared. . . ." Her tears had slowed. Now they returned full force at the idea of being abandoned.

"Look, I . . ." Slocum looked up the mountainside toward the lights of the Rice mansion and the comforts that waited for him there. The damn girl's tears were getting to him, though—her fear and the fact that he had accepted the wager from her late but unlamented owner. "Aw, shit," he said, "where's this cabin?"

Pearl brightened. "I'll show you, mister. I'll show you lots." She took him by the arm again, more gently this time, and began leading him back down the way they had come.

The cabin was log-walled and log-roofed, with the back and part of both sides being dug into the hillside. It was well below the camp, set in a pocket of rock almost down to the creek level below Howard's Tailings, and was completely hidden from view down there. Not even the sounds of the camp could reach them there, but the climb back up to the camp would have been hazardous as well as uncomfortable in bad weather, particularly through the winters.

Isolated as it was, though, the door was secured by a heavy padlock. Pearl unlocked it with a key taken from under a chunk of wood beside the door and went in ahead of Slocum to light a coal-oil lamp with a cracked chimney.

There was a single bed—which could have led to some interesting speculations about who had done what with whom during the tenure of the recently deceased Hank and

Wiley—a table, a stove, and some small crates for storage. The incompetent gamblers had not left much behind in the way of worldly possessions, and Slocum ignored the single bag that must have held their things.

"See, mister? Cozy."

"Yeah," Slocum grunted.

Pearl smiled. She seemed quite happy now that she was not alone. "I like it here. It's so much nicer than a hotel room with all them bugs to worry about. I ain't seen a single bug in here, not one. Got some mice, but they don't bother nothing. Some of them is almost like pets. I give them crumbs when Hank an' Wiley ain't watching. Wasn't, I mean." She giggled nervously. "Look do you wanta fuck now, or what?"

The blunt question was jarring, coming so close on the heels of her comments about the mice she fed. "Do you have anything to drink first?" Slocum asked.

"I think Wiley drunk the last of the bottle he brought down. I could look an' make sure."

"How about coffee? Do you have any of that?"

"Oh, sure. I could make you a good pot of coffee. I ain't much of a cook, but Tommy taught me to make coffee real good."

"Tommy?"

She frowned in deep thought. "Tommy was, oh, two or three fellers before Hank and Wiley, I think. Something like that."

"Did you do the same kinds of things for him that you did for Hank?" It was an idle question. Slocum sat on one of the crates that had been upended beside the table to serve as chairs and put his hat on the table.

"That's bad luck," Pearl said. She snatched the hat off the table and placed it carefully on a peg beside the door. "No, I just been doing shilling an' card spotting the last couple fellers. Tommy had a medicine show. I did some dancing for Tommy, out front, wearin' some veils an' such. Not much else. Then inside the wagon I'd do some more without all the veils. It got a pretty good draw, an' there was usually some high-roller that wanted more when that second dance was done. That was extra. I was pretty little then. Tommy always told the mark that I had to be pertected so he'd have to stay an' watch since I wasn't but twelve. Really I was fourteen, but the marks didn't know that. Anyway, the truth was that Tommy couldn't get it up the regular way.'' She was chattering over her shoulder while she bustled over the stove, putting water on for the coffee and trying to get a flame going out of the coals left from the last fire.

"He never used me at all himself. He just liked to watch the high-rollers while they was having their fun with me. There. That ol' fire is going now.'' She took a handful of roasted coffee beans from a cloth sack and brought them to the table to begin grinding them between a pair of flat stones. "Bein' with Tommy was pretty good. It was almost like having a regular daddy, maybe because he never fucked me or anything, but he come down sick with something one time an' sold me to another feller.'' She sounded quite matter-of-fact and unconcerned, as if being bought and sold was the most natural thing possible. Perhaps, Slocum thought, it was for her.

"How old are you now, Pearl?''

She shrugged. "Twenty, I think.''

She looked half again that age or more.

"What about your family?'' he asked.

She smiled at him. "Reckon you're my family now.''

He tried again. "I mean your real family. From back when you were little.''

"I don't rightly know. Can't remember that far back.''

She finished grinding the beans and dumped them into the pot of warming water to boil. "First thing I can remember is living in a big, cold old place with a bunch of other kids. Then a feller, an old geezer, but I don't recall his name, he come along and took me outta there. Said I was his then an' had to do whatever he wanted. What he wanted was to fuck a lot. Most every time he could get it up, which was a whole bunch when you figure how old he was. Anyhow, he fed me better than I was used to, an' I reckon I didn't mind none of it so much. But after a while he got kinda tired of me an' traded me off to another feller for a new plow and some other stuff. I been with movin'-along men ever since that time, one thing an' another. But I ain't *never* been alone. Never." Tears welled in her eyes anew at the thought of having to be alone.

"It's all right, Pearl. I won't leave you alone tonight."

She wiped her eyes and knelt beside him to lay her cheek on his knee. "I just knew you were a nice kind o' feller," she said.

Slocum sighed. He still did not know what in hell he was going to do with, or about, this girl. He was trying not to feel sorry for her, but he was not having a hell of a lot of success with it. "The coffee's boiling," he said.

Pearl's body was scrawny and loose. Her breasts were small, scarcely enough to fill a saucer, and they sagged. Her pubic hair—almost a novelty after being with Howard Rice's shaven ladies—was an abundant thatch of dark curls. She could have used a bath.

"You don't have to do this, you know," Slocum said.

"I don't mind, mister. Honest."

Slocum grunted and let the girl finish pulling his boots off. When she bent forward he could see that her back was scarred with small, crisscrossing lines of old wounds. Slocum leaned forward and ran his fingertips lightly over her back. "What happened there?" he asked.

She looked puzzled for a moment, then remembered. "Oh, that was a long time ago. I was with a feller, not for very long, who liked to take a stick to me. Punishment, he said it was, but I never could figure out what for. He'd whup me some an' then I'd have to suck him off. I ain't really liked to suck a feller ever since. I didn't like that feller." She looked up at him. "But I ain't refusing nothing you want me to do, mister. I know better'n that. I mean, if you want to whup me or whatever . . ."

"No," he said. "Nothing like that, Pearl."

She smiled up at him. She seemed grateful.

Slocum placed his Colt by the head of the bed and lay down. The blankets smelled of old sweat and other people, but he had slept in worse many times before. And he had promised the damn girl that he would not leave her alone tonight.

Pearl dipped a bit of rag into the warm dregs of the coffee she had fixed for Slocum and scrubbed herself vigorously. When she was clean enough to suit her, Pearl came naked to the bed and lay down beside Slocum. She seemed to expect no foreplay or preparations. Immediately she spread her legs apart and lay waiting for him to mount her.

In spite of himself—in spite of Pearl, too, for that matter—Slocum had a throbbing erection. There was something about the girl's total vulnerability and acceptance that aroused him. By her own belief, Pearl *belonged* to him. He could use her or abuse her in any way he might wish, and she would accept the treatment as his right.

Apparently thinking he might need help, Pearl reached

over and began to fondle him. When she felt the immense heft and length of him her eyes widened. "I never seen anybody that big," she said. She giggled. "Or that ready neither." She wriggled slightly and tugged on him to indicate he could mount her now.

"In a minute," Slocum said.

Surprising even himself, he put an arm around her and pulled her to him. Her body felt small and warm against his. He kissed her on the mouth.

Pearl's lips were slack and unresponding. When Slocum raised his head and looked at her, her eyes were wide and uncomprehending.

"Have you ever been kissed before?" he asked.

She thought for a moment. Finally she shook her head slowly from side to side. "I don't think so, mister." She smiled. "But it ain't bad, really."

He kissed her again. This time she inexpertly returned his kiss.

He ran his tongue inside her lips and over her teeth, probing until he found her tongue and played with it. Pearl pulled back away from him after a moment. "That really ain't bad, you know?"

"I know," Slocum said.

This time she kissed him, and her tongue was active, her lips mobile.

They lay in the embrace for a long time as Pearl tried out the new art of kissing. Eventually it seemed only natural that he roll on top of her and slide into her.

Even for a man of Slocum's exceptional size, her pussy was large and loose around his shaft, maintaining only a light touch around him and giving little pleasure except for its warmth.

Pearl clung to him and obviously wanted to continue the kissing while he mounted her, so he accommodated her.

He stroked in and out, getting little out of it himself. She seemed to be hardly aware of the penetration. All of her concentration was on the new experience of his kisses. Her hips lay limp and unresponsive while his massive cock probed deep inside her belly, but her lips were mobile and eager.

Pearl was actually, Slocum decided, quite lousy in bed.

After a time, though, the combination of her body warmth and the light friction that her over-stretched pussy was able to deliver melded to work their magic, and he felt himself building.

He disengaged from her mouth and began to pump more vigorously, trying to thrash his way to a climax inside the girl's unresponsive body.

Pearl lay under him quietly, accepting his near-frantic movement. She seemed to be uninvolved in the act.

Slocum was sweaty from his exertions. Eventually the hot, sweet flow built to the bursting point, and he gushed his juices out into her with a grunt of mingled effort and gratification.

He let his weight down on top of her. With a contented sigh that was almost a kittenish purr, Pearl searched for his mouth with hers and began once again to kiss him.

The next morning Slocum pulled his boots on, buckled the Colt at his waist, and stood to stamp his feet on the dirt floor and settle them into the boots. He picked up his hat.

"You ain't leaving me alone, are you, mister?"

"Damn it, Pearl, I . . ."

She closed her eyes and lowered her head, ready to meekly accept any blow or punishment he might choose to deliver.

"Aw, shit," Slocum said. "And you can start calling me John."

"Yes, John."

"I got to leave for a while. I have work to do. You can understand that, can't you?"

"Yes, John."

"Good. I'm going to go do that work now. Hell, Pearl, I don't know what to do about you."

"I could go with you," she suggested.

"No, damn it, you can't go with me." He was becoming disgusted, although whether with Pearl or with himself he could not have said. "Look, why don't you go shopping today." He had never yet met a female of any age who did not like to go out and buy things.

"I don't have no money," she said.

"I know that, Pearl. I'll give you some money. You can go shopping with it. Have yourself a fine time. You know?"

"What is it you want me to shop for?" she asked.

"Want? Hell, I don't *want* you to shop for anything. In particular, I mean. Just go . . . shop. You know. Buy something for yourself. A new dress, maybe. Whatever suits your fancy. A new dress would be nice, or a hat. Hell, I don't know what you'd like to have."

Pearl seemed to be having some difficulty understanding him. "You don't want anything?" she asked.

"No, I don't need anything."

"You want me to dress up special for you some way, then? Like the veils Tommy used to have me wear? Something so's you'll get it up easier?"

"No, damn it, I don't want you to get some kind of damn costume. I just thought you might enjoy going shopping. Just to buy yourself something pretty that *you'd* like to have."

"I never done anything like that before."

"Never?"

She shook her head. Her eyes were wide and innocent, and Slocum believed she was telling him the truth, as incredible as it seemed.

"Then it's about time you did. Here." He reached into his pocket and pulled out a fair portion of the amount he had taken from Hank Farloe the night before. "Take this. Go up to the stores and spend it any way you want. Get yourself something pretty, anything you'd like to have for yourself."

Pearl smiled. She looked like she could hardly believe her good fortune when she accepted the money from him. "It sounds like fun, mister. I mean John. You swear you don't mind?"

"Hell, no, I don't mind. It's my idea, remember?"

"You're *sure?*"

"Positive," he assured her.

"Golly, mister, I . . ."

"It's all right. Really. Enjoy yourself. I'll . . . uh, I don't know when I'll be back."

"You ain't—"

"I'll come back," he said quickly. "We'll work this out later. Meantime, I promise you I'll come back and we can talk it over then. Okay?"

She smiled. "An' I can buy anything I want? Anything at all?"

"Anything you like, Pearl."

She grinned and clung to him to give him a wet, well-practiced kiss.

"We'll do some more of that, too," he promised. He pulled her arms from around his neck and settled her heels back onto the floor. "Have yourself a good time today, Pearl. I'll see you later." Quickly he left the cabin, hurrying out into the cool air of the early morning.

When he was outside he felt almost as if he had made an escape. He shook his head in exasperation and hurried up the steep path toward the camp and Howard Rice's place.

13

Rice motioned Slocum to a seat in the tiny cubicle adjoining the Beulah Four's office. There was a knock on the door and Burl James looked in.

"You wanted to see me?" James asked Rice. The big man ignored Slocum.

"Come in, Burl. Shut the door behind you, please."

James did as he was asked and leaned back against the door with his arms folded across his chest.

"You can sit down, Burl," Rice said.

"I'll stand."

Slocum turned in his chair to give the security man a look that renewed his earlier promise to have it out with this bastard any time, any place. "I think Mr. James is afraid I might tarnish his reputation, Howard."

"I wish you two would try to get along better," Rice complained.

"You already know where I stand," James said. "I think you made an awful mistake bringing him in here. I think you've put the wolf into the henhouse, Mr. Rice. Don't be surprised when he cleans you out of eggs."

Slocum started to rise, but Rice stopped him. "John. Please." Slocum sat back down.

"I am aware of your feelings, Burl, but my decision is made. I trust John completely, and he is not a man who would betray that trust. I see no point in going over that same old ground now, though. You simply have to accept my judgement on the matter, Burl. That is not a suggestion. It is an instruction.''

Burl James looked like he was just busting from wanting to speak, but he held his tongue and was able to swallow whatever retorts he might have wanted to deliver. "Yes, sir," he grunted.

"The reason I asked the two of you to meet with me this morning," Rice went on, "is that I want to make an unscheduled shipment to the refinery."

"I don't think—" James began.

"Hear me out, Burl. We know that someone is planning to hit us in the near future. I think that has been quite thoroughly proven by the recent assaults on John's life."

"If you mean that poor damn freighter the other ni—"

"Burl! Quiet! I am well aware that you discount that as coincidence. It was not coincidence that someone tried to crush John with a falling rock on the path up to the mine. Someone has tried to kill him at least once, probably twice. The matter with the gamblers neither he nor I believes is connected, but there is even the faint possibility that that was set up. Regardless, the fact of a single deliberate assault confirms to me that someone wants John out of the picture here. That only reinforces my belief that he is the best person to help us with this problem, and I intend to act accordingly."

Rice paused to give James a stern look. He waited for the security man's nod of acceptance before he went on.

"Now. Opening that vug has meant a sudden and unexpected increase in the value of the shipments we are scheduled to make. I know your feelings on this, too, Burl, and I simply will not consent to your plan to send everything out in one huge, exceptionally well guarded train."

That was the first Slocum had heard about James's plan, probably because Rice had already rejected it and the proposal was not under consideration.

"The danger would be entirely too great," Rice said, "and the potential loss too difficult to bear in the event the robbers are successful. I still insist on a series of smaller shipments that would not beggar the Beulah Four if we fail to protect ourselves against these people."

"Yes, sir." Despite the words, James sounded like he was grumbling rather than agreeing with his employer.

"We will maintain the shipping schedule already decided on, but with an addition. I intend to add one concentrate shipment to that schedule. Today." Rice gave the two of them a tight smile. "I have been thinking that perhaps *un*scheduled shipments might help. Instead of going by a routine, we might be better off to ship on the spur of the moment, with no one but myself knowing when concentrate will be sent to the outside and, quite frankly, I would not decide myself when to make those shipments until I awaken in the morning."

"That might be effective," Slocum agreed. "If this robbery plan, whatever it is, involved more than a man or two, as Ferguson's warning suggests it must, it would be damn difficult to keep a full crew standing at the ready, waiting for you to take a notion to ship your concentrate."

"I disagree," James said. "I think you aren't being practical, Mr. Rice. I have to schedule the guards, you know, and I can't have all the men on duty all the time. That's what it would take to make this work. Why, every man we use has to be on duty when we're making a shipment or there wouldn't be enough people to guard the mule train and the concentrate vault at the same time. I have to juggle the schedules bad enough as it is, but if you make me try and keep people here around the clock, well, I just can't do it.''

"I thought of that, Burl, but we can always pay the men overtime. The shift coming off night duty can accompany the mules over the trail. Naturally they will receive overtime pay. Double the hourly rate. I doubt that any of them will object to the extra hours. And the men standing duty in the vault can extend their hours, also at double wages, until the first crew has returned and rested. That can be worked out, Burl. Trust me.''

"But—"

"The way I intend to find out if this is going to work, Burl, is to send a small concentrate shipment out.''

James scowled and asked, ''When?''

"Now.''

"Today?''

Rice nodded. ''I've already sent word for the mules to be brought around and packframes fitted. You can be loaded and on the trail in less than an hour.''

"But—"

"Do it, Burl. This could be important to all of us. Just do it.''

"Yes, sir.'' James did not look happy about it.

"No objections from you, John?'' Rice asked.

"No, I think it's a good idea myself,'' Slocum said.

"Do you feel up to riding with them?''

"Hell, I feel up to most anything,'' Slocum said. It was almost the truth. The ache in his ribs was still there, but it was nothing more than a lingering pain now, hardly worth admitting.

Rice chuckled. ''You must be at that. Catherine tells me you never did make it back to your room last night. The poor girl said she waited up for you half the night and finally fell asleep on your bed.''

The reminder that Slocum shared Rice's home as a guest made Burl James look like he wanted to bite someone, but the big man kept his silence.

Slocum laughed, but did not feel there was any need to give Howard an explanation about where or with whom he had spent the night.

There was another knock on the door and Ferguson's voice said, "Bill's here with the mules you ordered, Howard."

"Coming right out," Rice called. "Well, gentlemen, shall we forget our differences of opinion and get to work for the benefit of the Beulah Four?"

"You bet," Slocum said. He stood and moved swiftly across the floor to pull the door open. He was not particularly unhappy to note that James did not move aside quite quickly enough, and the door knocked the big man in the butt.

"Stay the hell away from me," James snarled. "Just stay the hell away, all right?"

Slocum taunted the man with a crooked grin and an exaggerated display of meek acceptance.

"Mr. Rice put me in charge of this train," James said, "so keep your nose outta things. If I want the advice of some damn outlaw I'll go find a better one than you and ask him."

Slocum laughed out loud.

"As a matter of fact, what I want you to do, *Mister* Slocum, is to *please* get the fuck to the back of the train and do your guarding back there. Least that way you might be of some possible use around here."

"Whatever you say, Mr. James," Slocum told him with another sarcastic grin. "I'm just an observer along for the ride."

They had already passed through Howard's Tailings and were approaching the start of the eyebrow trail to the outside world.

James was riding at the head of the train with two of his guards. Two more guards were posted at the rear of the long mule train.

Slocum had asked while the animals were being loaded why there were so many mules needed to carry such a relatively light shipment. He had been told that the extremely high center of gravity caused by perching the packs of concentrate over the mules' backs instead of hanging down at their sides made a normal load topheavy and unwieldy. Each mule could only carry a fraction of the weight it would be able to pack in regular panniers, and many more had to be used to transport the gold concentrate than would have been required for a trip over a wider trail.

Slocum had been given a small, wiry, dun-colored horse to ride. The saddle was borrowed too, his own being back at Rice's home, and the unfamiliar seat chafed the insides of his thighs. He shifted his weight, standing in the stirrups for a moment, and reined the horse to a slower pace so the pack train would pass by while he rode.

Up ahead, Burl James reached the start of the narrow trail and rode onto it, followed by the two guards. The mules, unbound and trained to doggedly follow one after another, plodded onto the trail one by one and were quickly lost to sight as they passed around the first of the many twists and bends on the slim ledge that was the trail.

Slocum pulled his horse to a halt. He could see no logical reason why he would be needed at the end of the procession since there were already two armed guards riding back there.

Howard Rice had told him that he would personally vouch for the loyalty of his guards. Besides, anyone dumb enough to attack the end of the pack train was too dumb to worry about. If an attack were launched back there, which would have to come from the Howard's Tailings end of the train, there would be nowhere for the robbers to go, even if they were successful. The guards up front could simply block the trail at the other end, and the robbers would be trapped between them and the camp. And miners generally are not considerate of people who are trying to steal the gold that would eventually reach their pockets in their pay envelopes.

No, Slocum thought, there would be no point in adding one gun back there.

He nudged his horse into the line of mules about midway between James and the rear guard.

The horse, apparently used to this passage, plodded forward as stolidly as any of the mules. It seemed not to notice the dropoff to the side nor to care about the hard, slick rock that scraped the side of Slocum's right stirrup.

Slocum, on the other hand, was not so happy to be crossing this trail again. It was inevitable, of course. Either that or live out the rest of his life in a small mining camp. But he did not *like* this trail, particularly after having gone over the edge the last time he rode it.

He was acutely conscious of the steep dropoff at his left and of how very few places there were where a man could comfortably climb down to the creek far below.

That was the same creek which ran near the cabin he had shared with Pearl the night before. Upstream its rumble had sounded soothing and pleasant through the night. Here, riding the scant trail so far above it, the sound of the water seemed menacing and ugly. Odd, he thought, how the same sound could take on such different meaning when the circumstances were altered.

They reached the first of the three indentations in the

wall and passed it, and Slocum was reminded of the plan he had had in mind when he came here.

He looked into the barren, rocky cut and saw nothing there but stone and trickling water. There was no sign, as of course he should have expected, of the cat or whatever it had been that spooked the Palouse.

A little farther ahead he reached the spot he had fallen from. The drop was too steep here and the creek too far below for him to see the carcass of the horse. He wondered where the man who had retrieved his gear had chosen to climb down and whether the man had any trouble bringing his things back up to the trail.

In spite of himself, Slocum found himself leaning toward the wall now and putting too much of his weight onto his right stirrup. Annoyed with himself for that, he sat upright in the unfamiliar saddle and willed himself to forget about things that were past.

They were nearing the second cut now, one of those where Slocum thought it was entirely possible the train could be tapped for several packs of concentrate.

He heard the sound of something grinding against the rock. The sound, possibly, of rock under an unwary foot, and his first thought was that it was that damned cat again, and he was going to go over the edge again.

He palmed his Colt and wondered if the borrowed horse would stand steady to gunfire. He should have asked but he had not, and it was too late to think about it now. If the animal reared, he was in trouble, and that was all there was to that.

Instead of a big cat, it was a man who stepped out onto the trail two mules in front of Slocum's horse.

"Howdy," Slocum said.

The man's head jerked around, and a wild-eyed look came into his frightened face. He groaned.

"Uh-huh," Slocum said. "You got company." The big .45 Colt was in Slocum's fist, pointing more or less toward the frightened man's midsection. "Funny," he said, "how a good idea gets around."

"I was just out huntin'," the man said.

Slocum had seen the fellow in Howard's Tailings in one of the saloons, but had not noticed him in particular.

"Hunting, huh? You can do better than that if you take the time to think about it. Hell, you'll have lots of time to work on your story while you're waiting for trial. If they go to the trouble. Might just hang you. I don't know."

The man swallowed. He looked decidedly pale now.

"You've still got the mules stopped," Slocum said. "Why don't you walk onto the other end of the trail an' we'll figure out what to do with you there."

The man bobbed his head nervously up and down and glanced over his shoulder before he started forward along the trail, trapped between one mule's back end and another's front.

As Slocum reached the opening to the cut where the man had been hidden the muzzle of his Colt swung to the side and he pulled the horse to a halt.

"You might as well come out too," he said conversationally.

"I'm alone," the man up ahead said.

"Uh-huh. So nobody will care if I put a bullet into that bit of blue cloth I see behind the rock over there." Slocum cocked the Colt. The sound of the hammer catching on the tempered steel sear was loud in the stillness around them.

Almost immediately a head popped up from behind the rock, and a hand appeared. The hand held a revolver.

Slocum snapped off his shot before the second would-be robber could fire. The slug took the robber in the forehead and jerked his head back. The dead man's fingers clenched convulsively around the trigger and the air was split by another gunshot.

Slocum's horse jiggered and danced, and for a moment Slocum thought he was going over the damned edge after all. But the horse calmed quickly and settled back down. Immediately ahead of Slocum, though, the mule he had been following lurched and slumped to its knees.

"Damn it, your partner's gone and shot that mule," Slocum said.

The live robber was pressed flat against the rock wall, obviously terrified that Slocum was going to shoot him too, or that one of the animals was going to bolt and knock him off the trail.

"I didn't . . ."

"I know."

The mule toppled sideways, leaning to the right, away from the dropoff with its last breath of life, and died there.

"I want you to do something," Slocum said.

"Yes, sir."

"Come back over here and shove that mule aside, or we'll be bottled up here."

"But . . ."

"Mister, the mule ain't going to feel it. The only other choice I got if you don't want to shove him over is for me to do it myself, and I don't figure to do that while you're standing there and might try to shoot me or something. So if I got to get down and shove that mule off the trail, I'm gonna have to drop you before I do it. Understand?"

The robber understood. He quickly stripped off his gunbelt and dropped it over the side, then crawled past the one mule between him and the dead animal.

He had difficulty getting leverage to shift the dead mule's weight, but he had more than enough reason to accomplish the job. And Slocum was in no particular hurry. Burl

James would be there whenever they reached the other end of the trail. Surely they would have heard the gunshots and would be alert and ready now, as would be the guards to the rear.

Eventually, wringing with sweat and thoroughly frazzled, the robber was able to tip the mule to the side enough that its own weight sent it plunging over the edge of the trail.

"See how easy that was?" Slocum said. "You can start walking now."

"Can't I rest some?"

"Sure. Soon as we get to the other end."

"I don't . . ."

Slocum cocked his Colt. The robber began walking. Slocum nudged the horse with his spurs, and within seconds the mule train was under way again.

14

Burl James glowered and growled quite a bit, but Slocum got the impression that the security man was not particularly interested in the robbery attempt. He listened to what Slocum had to say, but asked no questions, and when the cussing was subtracted all he really said to the captured robber was that he would be questioned later.

"We've wasted enough time here," James said not more than ten minutes after Slocum brought the prisoner out onto the flat where the trail opened out. "Randy, tie this bastard up and put him in the teamsters' shack over there. You boys take the train on. I'm gonna question this bird some an' then join you. Slocum, I want you to go back and get the pack that went over the side. You're a damn fool for letting it go, so it oughta be you that brings it back up. Time you get that done, we'll be too far ahead for you to catch us, so carry it back in to camp and we'll send it out again with the next shipment."

James stood with his hands on his hips, staring at Slocum as if to dare him to refuse the orders.

"All right," Slocum said mildly.

James looked almost disappointed that Slocum was not quarreling with him.

The guard named Randy took the robber into the shack and returned. He remounted, and the four guards moved the mule train slowly down the trail toward civilization—or what passed for civilization beyond Howard's Tailings.

"Are you going or not?" James demanded of Slocum.

"Whatever you say. Like you mentioned to me before, Howard put you in charge." Slocum touched his hat brim and reined the little dun back toward the miserable trail in to the camp.

As soon as he was out of sight of the shack, though, he stopped the horse and dismounted. He stripped its bridle and hung it on the saddle horn, then gave the animal a slap and sent it up the trail on its own. There was no way it could wander astray going in that direction, and when it reached the camp it was bound to be spotted and turned over to the Beulah Four.

Slocum was letting himself in for a walk, but there was something he wanted to see, and he had no place to stash the horse while he was going about it.

The horse plodded off and Slocum eased back to the end of the trail. There, instead of going out into the open, he began looking for handholds he could use to climb with. Five minutes later he was seated several hundred feet up on the mountainside with the end of the trail and the shack in view.

Slocum chuckled to himself quietly.

"Talk about wolves and henhouses," he muttered.

Burl James and the robber, whatever the man's name was, were coming out of the shack. The pair of them were getting on famously as far as Slocum could see. He was too far distant to hear what they were saying to each other, but they certainly seemed chummy. Both men were laughing, and they acted like old friends.

Which, Slocum thought, they probably were.

It was hardly a surprise. In fact, this or something very much like it was exactly what he had expected.

There were only three people who could have tipped the robbers to the last-minute decision to ship gold today. Slocum knew he had not done it. Howard certainly would not have. That left only Burl James to have given the word to a couple of his boys there in the camp.

Had Slocum been in James's shoes, he would have let this one go on through unmolested, but apparently the big man had decided that hitting this shipment would discourage any more spur-of-the-moment pack trains being sent out. Which obviously meant that he had something in mind for the big hit that had to be planned ahead of time and go according to a schedule.

Probably, Slocum mused, James would claim that someone must have seen the mule train being made up at the Beulah Four. Of course mule trains had to be made up for any shipment of any commodity, in or out of the camp, but with no other reasonable explanation, the argument might have held up.

Except for one little thing: Slocum being able to report James's friendliness with the robber was going to cause some pain for Howard Rice, but also some genuine security for the man.

It was also, Slocum thought, going to bring to a head this brewing business between himself and Mr. James down there.

Slocum admitted to himself that he was rather looking forward to that. He did not like Burl James worth a shit. Hadn't liked the man to begin with. Pinning the prick's ears back was going to be a real pleasure.

Slocum yawned and thought about lighting a cigar. Reluctantly he decided there was too much likelihood that one of the men below might see the smoke from it. He could wait another minute or two until they parted company.

James and the robber were still chatting, both men

smiling. Whatever they were discussing, they seemed to be in full agreement about it. James pointed to something behind the robber, then at the man's back. The robber turned and began dusting the seat of his trousers. He asked James something or said something to him.

James's response was to pull out his revolver and shoot his buddy in the back of the head.

The gunshot sounded oddly hollow from up on the rock above the men. The robber crumpled to the ground and lay there twitching for several minutes after he died.

Slocum frowned. He had not really expected that. He assumed that James would just report that his pal had escaped. Instead, the security chief was taking no chances at all. He used the time-honored technique of shooting first, then declaring an escape attempt.

Son of a bitch, Slocum thought. Too late to fret about it now, though. And the tough luck all belonged to that poor fool who had trusted Burl James.

Like Howard Rice, Slocum realized.

It was time to get back to Howard's Tailings and have a long talk with his host.

Slocum scrambled back down to the trail level and began hiking in toward the camp.

He looked down at the dead mule and considered for a moment. The animal's pack was still lashed to the packframe, and anyone who had seen a shipment of concentrate leaving the Beulah Four in the past was almost certain to recognize the sack for what it was.

Slocum was not especially fond of climbing, particularly now that that last climb had set his ribs to aching again, but he had told Howard he would help protect his mine's profits, and right down there was a bagful of gold concentrate waiting for the next passerby to come down and collect it.

He lighted the cigar he had been wanting before and took another look below the trail.

This was one of the places he had considered using himself, and the slope here was steep but hardly sheer. It was certainly climbable, as Slocum had intended when he chose it with his own theft in mind.

Of course, his intention then had not been to lug a sack of gold concentrate back up to the trail and then tote the damn thing the rest of the way back to the camp afoot. That, he thought, was asking a bit much.

Still, he could go down and hide the bag. That would probably protect it, he thought. Then Howard could send a man out to get it, as he had sent the man to bring in Slocum's gear. That way it could be done with a mule or a horse to carry the concentrate.

Uh-huh, Slocum thought. There was even room enough up here on the trail for a mule to turn around where the cut was.

He wondered if Howard would want the dead robber—the first dead robber, that is—brought in, too. If so, that was his business. Slocum had seen enough dead men that he did not feel any compulsion to examine another. He began the slow climb down to the creek and the mule with its valuable cargo of unrefined gold concentrate.

He reached the bottom without mishap and sat on a rock long enough to smoke another stogie. Between the altitude and the fall several days previously he was feeling out of shape and quite frankly needed the rest.

He finished his smoke and flipped the cigar butt into the leaping white water of the racing creek.

A few quick strokes of his knife and the sack of gold was free of the packframe. Slocum picked it up. It was a heavy son of a buck. For a mule it was no burden at all. A decently built mule could comfortably handle three hundred pounds of freight. This sack weighed only fifty pounds or so. But it was all dead weight. Slocum was damn well convinced he had made the right decision about hiding the gold instead of trying to carry it back to Howard's Tailings by himself.

He balanced the sack on his shoulder and looked around, searching for a place where it could keep safe but that he would be able to describe well enough for someone else to find it.

Over there, he thought.

Something that felt like a hard-thrown brickbat smashed into the side of his head.

He felt his knees buckle.

He knew he was falling. He fought against it, trying not to go down, but not even sure why he should care if he fell or not.

He was dimly aware that the concentrate sack had tumbled off his shoulder, and he was reeling forward on wobbly legs, trying to keep to his feet and knowing even as he did so that he could not possibly stay upright. Not with his head spinning and his ears roaring. He was going down, and that was all there was to that.

He heard a second gunshot. *Second?* he asked himself. That seemed right, although he did not now remember having heard the first. Then he was falling forward.

Cold water engulfed him. It was like being plunged naked into a snowbank, the way a crazy Finn had talked him into doing one time.

But that time he had been able to breathe. This time when he tried to breathe he got a mouthful of shockingly cold water instead.

His arms flailed at the white foam that surrounded him,

and his ears were filled with the roar of the cascading water.

An impossibly strong current grabbed him and shook him like a terrier would a rat, and he was yanked underneath the surface of the stormy stream.

Drowning, he thought. *Battered.*

The current smashed him against an underwater rock, and fresh pain lanced through his ribs.

The pain forced a yell from his throat, but all that came out were bubbles.

Gravel and stone scraped harshly over his arms and knees, and he felt himself being bumped along the bottom of the raging creek.

He tried to fight back, to claw his way back into the world of air and warmth and sunshine. But all he could feel now was hard rock and the icy grip of the roaring, irresistible flow of water.

Then he could feel nothing at all.

He could see nothing, he could feel nothing. It was like he was floating on a cool, chill cloud.

And then there was nothing at all.

15

Slocum's eyes fluttered but did not open. He did not think he had the strength to open them. He was not sure he ever would have again.

For that matter, he was not sure he was still alive *to* open them.

He gave that some thought and concluded that he must be alive. He was so cold his damn teeth were chattering, and he was about to shake himself to pieces from shivering. That, he thought, must be proof positive that he was alive. When he died he was going to be hot, not cold. At least, everything he had ever heard on that subject led him to believe it was fire and brimstone that was coming his way.

So now he must still be alive.

But, Lordy, he was cold.

He managed to get his eyes open after all.

He was still in the water. No wonder he was so terribly cold. He was lying on his back in a pool of softly swirling ice water. He looked around. He was caught in an eddy. A few feet away he could see and hear the roaring, crashing boil of white water that was the runoff-swollen creek. He had no idea how he had gotten into this eddy, but he knew that if he had not floated or crawled or drifted in here he would certainly be dead now.

He shook his head. It hurt something awful. Now he remembered. He had been shot.

He reached a hand up and lightly touched the side of his head. There was a furrow in the flesh there where none had existed before, and a small flap of loose skin hung down over his ear.

No wonder his head hurt so bad, he thought.

It also hurt for him to move his elbow. His arms and legs were abraded by hard stone that had been like sandpaper on his skin when the creek bounced and tumbled him downstream in its grip.

He did not seem to be bleeding, though, he concluded after some examination. The cold and the water had combined to wash his wounds and to minimize the flow of blood near the surface of his skin.

Cold. Reminded, he began shivering again.

Painfully, slowly, he began to assume control over his limbs. With great care he dragged himself to the edge of the eddy pool. He tried to get up and walk out of the water, but he could not make his legs respond. All he could manage to do was to get his chest up onto the rocks beside the stream. Even that felt heavenly, and the small gain pleased and strengthened him.

Lift and lurch, he told himself. Up with the arms just a little bit and flop forward. He tried it and gained another few inches.

He was dizzy and his head hurt abominably. It would have been easy to quit, to give up and lie there quietly until the water swept away the last warmth from his body and he died from exposure. It would have been easy—comfortable, too—but he was not tempted.

He might have been tempted except for one thing. Whoever had shot him—Burl James, probably—was still alive. Slocum could not quit as long as that was so.

He tried again. This time he was on dry land almost to his waist. It seemed a great and wonderful accomplishment.

You son of a bitch, Slocum silently told the rifleman who had shot him, *you figure you got me, but you've fucked up for fair now. Because next time it's my turn.*

He levered himself up and out again, and most of his torso was out of the water. The sharp rocks cut into his gut, adding to his discomfort, but he did not mind. The pain reminded him that he was alive and that he had a score to settle, a debt to collect. He did not intend to let that debt go unpaid.

Once more, he told himself.

He heaved against the rocks again, rolled over, and was finally, completely, on dry land.

Slocum grinned. It was a chilling expression that promised vengeance of the rawest kind, and it warmed him in the deepest pits of his inner resources.

With a strength that came from sheer determination and nothing more, John Slocum dragged himself away from the creek and across the several yards that separated him from the shelter of a huge, fallen spruce.

He burrowed into the decomposed needles that had been left on the ground there, and he felt almost warm even though his teeth were still chattering uncontrollably.

He rolled onto his back and tried to figure out where he was.

The trail to Howard's Tailings was still overhead, so he had not been swept the full length of the canyon. Opposite him, across the creek, there was a fan-shaped spill of broken rock, and a thin line of water flowed down to join the creek. It must have been that flow, rushing at its wildest, that had carved out the pocket in the creek bed where the eddy had formed.

So he was at the foot of one of the cuts. He had climbed

down the second cut. So this was the first. It had to be, he reasoned.

Which meant he had a hell of a long way to travel to get back to Howard's Tailings.

He tried to sit up, intent on starting that journey, but he had used very nearly the last of his resources. He had nothing left to go on and could not even raise himself to a sitting position. He fell back exhausted against the crumbling bed of needles.

He must have slept, because the next time he opened his eyes it was dark, and he felt colder than he could ever remember feeling in a hard lifetime.

This time, though, he was able to sit up. He fumbled in his pocket for matches and struck one. There was no flame. It was with great difficulty that he was able to figure out that the matches had been immersed in water and would no longer strike.

He cursed a little, reconsidered, and cursed a lot. It seemed to help. If nothing else, it made him feel better.

What he needed was a fire. Badly needed. But there was no way he could make a fire. He might have managed one if he had the strength to walk around and find some flint. But, damn it, if he was able to do that he would not need the fire. He could just get up and head upstream toward Howard's Tailings.

He tried another match. It was as useless as the first had been.

He tried every match he had. None of them would strike. He cursed some more. This time it did not make him feel the least bit better.

Disgruntled and discouraged, Slocum swept the ground with his hands, gathering together all of the decomposed spruce needles he could reach and pulling them into a pile.

He shaped the pile like a mounded grave, a similarity

that struck him with bitter irony as he finished putting it together. Then, finally, he lay beside the long mound and began scooping it over himself, first over his legs as he sat up so he could reach that low, then higher. He buried himself in ancient needles and dirt, at the end using one hand and burying all of himself but his face. Then he pulled that hand in until the crushed needles and thin soil covered him completely except for his nose.

With a sigh John Slocum lay back and tried to ignore the lingering cold until his meager body heat had a chance to do its job and warm this pile of refuse that could become his coffin.

The first rays of sun woke him. He lay for a long time in his cocoon of spruce needles, enjoying the warmth of them after the cold, cold water.

Later, when the warming rays of the sun reached the bottom of the canyon where he lay, he rolled out of the nest of needles and let the sun add its heat to his battered body.

His clothing was in tatters. He would have to go to the house, he thought, to get his other clothes. By now Catherine should have them ready for him.

Then a thought struck him, and he wondered if it would be safe to go to Howard Rice's house.

By now Burl James would have had more than enough time to return to the camp. He would have had ample opportunity to spin a tale for Howard's ears.

He could not give Howard the explanation that Slocum had been killed in the robbery attempt, because the guards had seen Slocum afterward. And they were not in on the plan themselves, or James would not have sent them ahead. He could simply have pulled down on Slocum and gotten the guards to go along with a story about Slocum trying to rob the shipment. There would not have been any need then to shoot his own partner.

So the guards apparently deserved the faith Howard placed in them. It was only James, or at worst a few of the Beulah Four guards, who had joined the man in whatever his plan was now.

If Slocum was any judge, then, even believing him dead, Burl James would have come up with some story that would place Slocum at fault. Something that would cast doubt on Rice's trust of Slocum.

He thought about that while he lay in the sun.

That sack of gold concentrate, he thought. He had been holding that when James shot him. He had had it on his shoulder and dropped it. James would have seen that.

Slocum was almost certain that when he reached the second cut, across from the dead mule, there would be no bag of valuable concentrate on the ground over there.

James's greed and hatred would have seen to that. The man had a chance there to steal for himself a sack of Howard Rice's gold, keep it, and place the blame on John Slocum.

Of course. He would not have to say anything about Slocum being shot. Just that he had sent Slocum back to retrieve the gold and return it to the camp.

When Slocum and the gold both disappeared, the logical assumption would be that John Slocum had stolen the concentrate and left.

Saying nothing, Burl James would be able to tell the cleverest lie of all.

The proof of the pudding would be if he found no sack of gold lying beside the creek up there.

Slocum stood, ignoring the pain the movement cost him, and began the slow walk upstream toward Howard's Tailings.

At the next cut, high above him over the trail there, he found the dead mule.

There was no sack of gold concentrate.

Smiling thinly to himself, eager to have a word or three with a gentleman named James, Slocum continued his slow, painful progress upstream.

16

The last mile and a half Slocum had to stop every hundred yards to rest. Then more often. Toward the end he was dizzy and kept falling down, and he crawled the last hundred yards on his hands and knees.

He was barely able to remember his name much less achieve coherent thought, but somehow he found his way to the door of the cabin where Hank and Wiley had lived.

It was already dark, and there was a light on inside. Hoping Pearl was in there, knowing that regardless of who it was he had to get food and rest and warmth or die from exposure to the elements in his weakened condition, he crawled to the door and collapsed against it. He barely had strength enough left to tap his knuckles against the weathered wood.

"Who's there?"

Slocum felt relieved. It was Pearl's voice. "John," he croaked.

"Who?"

"John, damn it. Now open this door and get me inside, woman." A flush of quick anger put heat in his words and gave him the strength to speak up.

He heard the girl's footsteps rushing to the door. She yanked it open and was crying and bawling before she could bend down to him. "Johnny, ohmagawd, Johnny, I was *alone* last night. All alone. I never been so scared in my whole life, I swear. An' I thought you was gonna leave me alone tonight, too. I just couldn'ta stood it, Johnny, I swear I couldn't.''

She kept blubbering on like that, but she dragged him inside and finally seemed to realize that all was not quite as it should be with him.

''Johnny? What happened to you, Johnny?''

''Shut up, Pearl,'' Slocum said wearily, ''and fix me something to eat.''

''Sure, Johnny. Whatever you want. You know I'll do whatever you want.'' She left him where he was on the floor and turned toward the stove.

''Damn it, Pearl, wait a minute. Get me up onto the bed first. Then fix something to eat.''

''Sure, Johnny, anything you say.''

She helped him off the floor and onto the bed and again turned to the stove. She already had a fire going. She put a pot of water on top of the stove and began dumping things into it. Slocum thought he saw some potatoes tossed in and several chunks of dubious-appearing meat. He was not sure what else.

''Help me out of these clothes, Pearl.''

Misunderstanding, she smiled at him and first began to take off her dress.

''No, damn it, I'm half dead and I ain't interested in that right now. I wanta get out of these rags and get wrapped up in a blanket or something to get warm. Is that coffee I see on the stove there?''

''No, Johnny, that's a pot of tea I made for myself. But I can fix you some coffee real quick.''

Pearl seemed to be having some difficulty accepting the situation. That, Slocum thought, was absolutely the most charitable way it could be put. The girl was willing enough, to be sure, but he was beginning to get the idea that she was even less bright than he had thought. Or maybe she just could not handle any kind of crisis. Whatever, he was going to have to be careful to make allowances for some deficiencies here and tell her things slowly and one thing at a time.

"Pour me some of the tea, Pearl," he said.

She quickly got a cup—not a clean one, he noticed—and poured dark fluid into it.

The tea had been steeped until it was as black as coffee, and there were bitter leaves floating all through the horrid brew. Tommy should have taught her how to make tea while he was giving her the instructions about coffee, Slocum thought.

Still, it was hot and it was stout, and he could feel the warmth from it flowing through him almost as soon as he drank it. He finished that cup, straining the leaves out as best he could with his teeth and spitting out what he missed that way, and asked for another.

"Sure, Johnny."

"Pearl."

"Yes, Johnny?"

"Please don't call me Johnny any more. It sounds sorta strange the way you say it. Call me John instead, okay?"

"Sure, whatever you say, Johnny. I mean John. Anything you want." She gave him a quavering smile. "You ain't gonna make me stay alone again tonight, are you, John?"

He lay back against the wall at the head of the bed, weariness seeping through him, but at least feeling a little warmer after the terrible tea. "No, Pearl, I won't leave you here alone tonight."

"Oh, John!" She jumped up so quickly that Slocum

thought something was wrong. He jerked upright to a sitting position, automatically reaching for his Colt.

"I got to show you, John. It's the most wonderfulest thing you ever seen, John, I swear it is."

Slocum relaxed. Pearl was excited, not frightened. She dashed to a back corner of the cabin and opened the lid of one of the storage crates.

"See here, John?"

She reached into the box and tenderly, almost with awe, lifted out a pasteboard box that she had wrapped in an old cloth to protect it.

"What is it, Pearl?"

"It's what I bought yesterday, John. What you bought for me, I mean." She gave him a smile of great joy.

Reverently, Pearl unwrapped the box and removed its lid. She wiped her hands carefully on the skirt of her dress before she reached in and brought the contents of the box out for him to see.

It was a hat, a lady's hat made of green velvet, with a clutch of iridescent pheasant feathers streaming out behind it and some other foofaraw mixed in there that Slocum did not recognize.

"Ain't this the grandest thing you ever seen, Johnny?"

"Pearl."

The joy and the excitement disappaered at the sound of his stern tone of voice. "Did I do wrong, Johnny? Do I hafta take it back?"

"Oh, Pearl. Damn it, girl, what am I gonna do with you?" He held out his arms and motioned her to him. She came, holding the precious hat gingerly, as if she expected him to snatch it away from her.

He pulled her down and petted her some and soothed her. "I didn't mean that, Pearl. The hat is just about the prettiest hat I ever did see. I was saying your name that way because you forgot and called me Johnny again. That's all, Pearl. Of course you can keep your hat." He kissed her lightly, and her face brightened with a childlike pleasure. "Try it on for me, Pearl. I have to see how it looks on you."

Excited again, she bounced away from the bed and put the hat on. Slocum was surprised. It actually looked quite good on her. In fact, if it were not for her shabby and rather dirty dress, and perhaps with something suitable done to her hair, she would have looked damn well attractive.

"It's beautiful, Pearl. It is probably the most beautiful hat I ever saw, and you wear it very well."

She beamed.

"Pearl."

"Yes, Johnn . . . ngh." She managed to bite the last sound off before it was completely out of her mouth.

"The pot is boiling over, Pearl."

She leaped to the stove and pulled the pot aside, then went back to the table and lovingly replaced her beautiful hat in its box before she did anything else about their dinner.

When she did serve the meal, it was worse than the tea had been. The potatoes had been neither washed nor peeled, and the meat, whatever it was, was a rubbery, disgusting mess. The other things she had tossed in turned out to be beans, and they had not begun to cook long enough to soften. It was like chewing pellets of half-baked clay. Still, it was the first food he had tasted in two days, and it was hot, and he was hungry enough to get it down and ask for seconds. That seemed to please Pearl almost as much as his admiration of her hat had done.

Later, when Pearl stripped to join him in the bed, he noticed a saucer-sized bruise on her hip.

"What's that?"

She looked where he was pointing and shrugged as if it was of no consequence. "I got kicked."

"By what, a mule?"

She shook her head shyly.

"What happened?"

"Don't know that I oughta tell you."

"Tell me."

She lowered her eyes, unwilling to look at him directly. "While you was gone, see, I figgered you wasn't coming back for me. An' I figgered I'd have to do something to keep myself. An' I didn' have money enough after buying my pretty hat to get me a crib, so I seen this bunch of gentlemen." She paused. "Are you sure you don't mind hearin' this?"

"Tell me," he said again.

"Well, I seen this whole bunch of gentlemen. An' I figgered one of them fellers might want to fuck. So I went over to them and asked. And this big feller that was in charge of them, he kicked me. Told me they was busy and I had to get outta there or he'd do worse'n that. So I got."

"A big man, huh?"

She nodded. "Mr. James. He played cards with Hank a time or two, and I didn't think he'd be so bad, but I reckon he didn't recognize me or something, 'cause he got real mad."

James. Slocum might have guessed. "Do you know what Mr. James was doing with those men, Pearl?"

She shrugged. "I'm not sure. Something to do with hiring a whole bunch more guards for the mine up there. They're gettin' really funny about it. I mean, it's one thing to guard somethin'. But these fellers, they're all over now. Up at the mine an' down at the big boss's house. I don't know his name, but I know which place is his 'cause it's so big and grand and everything. Now there's guards all over it. A bunch of fellers mostly that I ain't seen around here before. They come in this morning an' went right to work. And some of them are mean. I'm kinda glad that Mr. James didn't let me ask none of them if they wanted to fuck, because they look like the kind that'd do it an' then not pay. And like they'd want to hurt a girl, too." She made a face and shuddered.

Slocum lay back and closed his eyes. Damn well interesting, he thought. James had had the time to fill Howard in with some lies and some misdirection. And now it seemed he was using that as an excuse to beef up the security force with a bunch of new men of his own choosing.

Hell, Slocum had played right into the bastard's hands. Not intentionally, by any means, but it had worked out that way.

"There aren't any cigars around here, are there?" he asked. It had been almost two days since he had had a smoke, too, and he was really wanting one.

"Hank smoked. I can see if there's any in his stuff."

Slocum nodded and closed his eyes again. There had to be some way to turn Burl James's plan against him. The question was what that way might be.

In a moment Pearl was at his side with two dried-out cigars and a match. She lighted a cigar for him and blew out the match.

"Thanks," he said.

"You don't hafta thank me. I'll do anything for you, John. Anything at all." She crept onto the bed at his side and snuggled happily against him. "When you get done smoking, John, could we maybe kiss a little again? I liked that."

"Sure, Pearl. We can kiss a whole lot if you want."

She smiled.

Slocum would not have thought it possible—he was sure he was too tired and too sore and too worried with Howard Rice's problems to allow room for such thoughts—but with Pearl snuggled puppy-warm against him, he could feel that familiar, pleasant urge building low in his crotch.

He reached for her and cupped one flabby breast in his hand while he finished the cigar.

Pearl sighed happily as he bent to kiss her, and she spread herself open for him.

She was no better at it this time than she had been before, not from a lack of willingness but from a basic disinterest, but at least she was there. Slocum got off as quickly as he could and was asleep almost as soon as he had rolled off her.

17

He woke as the first light of dawn was filtering through the cracks in the log walls. The walls needed rechinking before the next winter, he thought lazily, still half asleep.

When he moved he came fully awake, small, sharp pains needling into his consciousness from every part of his body. For a change it was not his ribs that hurt the worst, although they were still bad. For a change it was the many small scrapes and abrasions caused by being tumbled over the rocks and gravel in the force of the swift-flowing water that hurt the most. He gritted his teeth and ignored the many hurts, sitting up and reaching for a cigar.

His motion woke Pearl at his side. She blinked and looked up at him through heavy, puffy eyelids.

Slocum lighted the second and last of the cigars she had found for him, drew the smoke deep into his lungs, and exhaled. He bent and kissed the girl, remembering the promise he had made to her last night but had not been able to stay awake to keep then. Pearl snuggled happily against him and went about the enjoyable task of kissing him back. "Nice," she murmured against his lips.

"Good."

"You know, John, I think I like you better'n any feller I've ever been with."

"Thank you, Pearl." It must have been intended as a compliment; he accepted it as one.

He felt a rise of quick, insistent pressure at his groin and came to a hard erection. Pearl must have felt it bumping against her belly because after a moment she moved aside to accommodate him and reached between them to run her fingers up and down his shaft while she continued to kiss him.

Slocum wanted her, but she was really a lousy lay. He wanted something better than Pearl was able to give him.

"You told me once that you don't like to suck cock," he said.

Pearl nodded sleepily and tried to nuzzle closer to kiss him again, but he pulled back from her slightly and petted her head so it would not seem that he was rejecting her.

"You do it, but you don't particularly like it, is that it?" he asked.

She shrugged.

"Try it," he said.

He was really expecting a refusal. But not from Pearl, not from this girl who was so used to being dominated that she accepted domination as the right and proper way of things. She did not even frown, but just slipped lower in the bed until she was poised over his throbbing cock.

She wet her lips and touched him all over with her fingers, peering at him like a sculptor examining a block of marble before approaching it with hammer and chisel.

After a moment she bent to him.

Her mouth was as mobile as her hips were inert, her lips as greedily efficient as her pussy was limp.

She gobbled him deep, shoving and pushing and grunting with effort as she fought to capture all of him in her mouth and throat.

Big as he was, Slocum was almost afraid he would tear

her lungs out, but she was on top and had control of the situation. She could pull back any time she was hurt.

She did not pull back. She pushed and grunted and forced her mouth down over him like a hot, tight, dripping wet sleeve of taut-stretched rubber until her nose was buried in the hair on his balls and her chin gouged sharply into his lower belly.

Then, once she was able to accommodate all of him, she began to pump up and down on him, her head moving so fast that her hair bounced and flew, the cheeks of her ass shaking and quivering with her rapid-fire efforts.

Through it all, upstroke or down, she continued to suck as hard as she was capable of doing, pulling at him like a mighty, steam-driven pump, demanding the release of his come, feverishly working to pull the hot juices into her mouth.

Slocum was convinced if the bed dropped out from under him, the force of her sucking would be enough to keep him suspended in midair, dangling from her busy mouth like a dead mouse being carried by a hunting cat.

All the while she sucked him she teased his bloated sack with mobile fingers, spreading the sensation throughout his groin until it was so good it was almost unbearable.

Without warning he erupted into her, spurting in a flow that seemed endless.

Slocum grunted and strained, driving himself deeper into her throat. Her throat tightened and rippled against him as she swallowed, increasing the sensation she was giving him and bringing still more white-hot come bursting out of him. He grabbed the back of her head and pushed her down onto his exploding shaft until the sharp jab of her chin hurt his gut, but even then he would not release her.

Finally, the fiery waves of pleasure exhausted, he released her and lay back on the rumpled bed.

Still Pearl continued to suck and pull at his limp flesh until she had captured the last possible drop of salty fluid from his loins.

Slowly, gently, she lifted her head and disengaged herself from him. She petted his flaccid cock and kissed it lightly.

When she turned to look at him she had a worried expression on her face. "Are you gonna hit me?"

"Hit you? Of course I'm not going to hit you. That was . . . that was about the best I've ever had that way, Pearl. You're terrific."

She looked relieved and pleased. "That other feller, he hit me a lot when I wasn't good enough. He taught me how he liked it an' I tried to do it good, but he gen'r'ly hit me when I was done."

Slocum pulled her to him and stroked and cuddled her. "You were very, very good," he told her over and over again.

And it was the truth. She was an absolutely terrible fuck, but she could give a better French job than Lynnanne or Catherine or damn near anyone.

"You're wonderful," he told her again.

Pearl beamed. It was obvious that she was not used to receiving compliments, and the sound of them to her was like candy to a child. She glowed with his praise and reached down to fondle him again.

"Ya know," she said, "I didn' mind doing you, Johnny. Oh. Sorry. I shoulda said John. Please don't be mad at me."

"I'm not mad, Pearl. And I'm glad you didn't mind it. You were marvelous."

She smiled and sighed. "If I go wash my mouth out, would you kiss me some more, maybe?"

"Sure, honey. I'll do that. And while you're up, put us

a pot of coffee on. A cup of your coffee would be real nice now.''

Pearl smiled and gave him a quick, hard hug before she scampered out of the bed and skipped naked across the small room to start the fire and get the water on for coffee.

Slocum watched her, aware of the thick bush of her pubic hair and the looseness of her skinny body. She was tall but, except for her height, and that abundant thatch of hair, she still could almost pass for being a kid in her early teens.

He looked at her hazily, and an idea began to form.

"After breakfast," he said, "there are some things I want you to do for me, Pearl."

"Anything, John. You know I'd do anything for you."

Pearl returned in mid-afternoon. She was beaming with pride and pleasure and looked like a different woman in her new finery. Her arms were loaded with packages, including one long, thin, cloth-wrapped bundle.

"Oh, John, don't I look grand? The ladies at the store, they said I look grand. They let me look in a mirror, too, a real big mirror. It most took my breath away, I swear it did. I couldn' hardly believe it, I looked so grand in that big mirror."

"They were telling you the truth, Pearl. You look like a regular lady in that gown."

The green velvet gown was quite obviously a mate to the hat she had already purchased, and she put her packages down and ran immediately to fetch the hat from its protected storage.

When she put it on, Slocum had to admit that she looked quite fine indeed. Presentable in any company. Until she opened her mouth to speak. Still, for what he wanted of her, she was dressed to perfection now, and he told her so.

She preened and pirouetted in front of him, basking in his admiration for her.

"Even your hair looks different, Pearl."

She giggled and said, "One o' the ladies at the store told me I oughta look extra good in this fine dress an' said she'd show me how to fix my hair like this. She showed me in a mirror so's now I can do it up this way any time I want. Do you really like it, John, *really* like it?"

"I really and truly like it that way, Pearl."

"Oh, I remembered to get you your cigars, like you asked me to. An' matches. I think I 'membered everything you asked for, John."

Slocum was willing to believe that. Pearl seemed to have an excellent memory. Once she learned something, she did not forget it. She seemed to have some difficulty figuring things out for herself but no trouble at all remembering them once learned. It was a shame, he thought, that no one had ever taken the trouble to teach her how to screw.

Not that she would be unable to learn now. He wondered if he should try to teach her. Probably there would be no time for that. Not with what he had in mind here. That was a pity. In the past she most likely had just been spread open and used, casually and with little concern, so she had never learned about the ways a woman could please a man—or be pleased by one.

That was a shame, Slocum thought. On the other hand, it was a real blessing that someone had bothered to give her French lessons. That she had learned extraordinarily well. And that, he thought, was going to come in damned handy now.

Pearl unwrapped the packages on the table, opening and

displaying them one by one, relating to him the circumstances and the pride of each purchase.

There was coffee, tinned meat, fresh-baked bread, and a small tin of corn syrup.

There were lacy underthings for Pearl and a complete set of clothing for Slocum to replace the rags he had been wearing when he came out of the creek.

A box of cartridges for his .45 Colt and another, larger box of ammunition.

There were several sheets of paper and a lead pencil.

A razor, mug, and lump of shaving soap.

Finally she handed him the long, heavy bundle she had had so much trouble carrying down the steep path from the camp above.

Slocum unwrapped it.

"I hope you ain't mad, John. I know it ain't what you told me to get, but the man at the store said he didn' have none of those an' this here was the very best he did have."

Instead of the Winchester repeater he had told her to buy, she had brought a single-shot Sharps with flecks of rust on the long, octagonal barrel. It was chambered for the .50-90 cartridge, which she had also bought. Slightly too light a load for buffalo hunting down on the plains and much too slow to fire for serious fighting, it was just the thing needed for bringing down elk in these high mountains.

"He said it was the best he had," Pearl said again uncertainly. "Are you mad, John?"

"No, I'm not mad at you, Pearl."

"You're sure, ain't you, John? I mean, I spent an awful lot o' money. I swear, I never handled so much money before in my life. It kinda scared me. But you said it was all right. It is all right, ain't it, John?"

"You did just fine, Pearl. I couldn't have done any better myself. Honestly I couldn't."

She smiled. "I did good, then."

"You did real good, Pearl." He rewarded her with a kiss, which led to more kisses, and then to the removal of the handsome new green dress.

"Leave the pretty hat on, Pearl."

"Yeah?"

"Uh-huh. And get down right over here. I want to make sure you haven't forgotten anything since this morning."

"Sure."

"You won't mind now?"

She shook her head. "Not no more, I don't think. You ain't the kind to hit a girl. I won't mind doing you again that way."

Whether she really minded it or not, Slocum discovered that she was indeed as good as he remembered. Possibly better. It was a wonder her head did not blow off, he came so hard. Or that his did not burst from the force of the explosion she brought him to.

When she was done she rocked back on her heels and smiled up at him. He was sitting on the edge of the bed with his new jeans dropped around his ankles. "Was I good, John?"

"You were wonderful, Pearl."

She sighed and smiled.

"Go wash your teeth, Pearl."

She jumped up happily. "Can we kiss some more?"

"You bet. For just a minute, though. And put some water on the stove to heat. I want to shave."

After supper, by the light of the single lamp in the small cabin, Slocum shaved. When he was done, he put a fresh dollop of water into the mug and began making more lather.

"I don't suppose you've ever learned how to use a razor?" he asked.

"No. D'you want me to?"

"There isn't time now, Pearl. Come over here and take your dress off."

"Sure." She accepted his instructions without comment and within seconds was naked.

"I want you to sit on the side of the table, Pearl."

"Gee, I never done it that way before."

Slocum laughed. "What I have in mind is something I've never done before either. But we might get around to the other in a few minutes too. Hop up here, now."

Pearl did as she was told, and Slocum took a seat on the upended crate, sitting between her wide-spread thighs.

Damn, he thought. After all these years and all the scrapes and shenanigans he had gotten himself into, he had been almost certain there was nothing that he had not already experienced. Well, this right here was a new one for him.

He reached for the lather mug and began to plaster Pearl's crotch with creamy white soap.

She giggled. "That tickles."

"Hold still, damn it. I don't want to cut you."

"Oooh! It *tickles,* John. An' it's so *cold.*"

"Hold still, girl. I can't send you off visiting my friend all cut up." He dragged the honed and stropped feather edge of the straight razor through the first wiry curls of Pearl's thick hair.

"Ouch."

"Sorry. Now hold still." His face set in hard, careful concentration, tongue poking at the corner of his mouth, the tall, rugged outlaw bent himself to the task of shaving Pearl's pussy.

18

Dawn found Slocum high on the rim above the trail leading out of Howard's Tailings. The climb had been hellish in the darkness, not just because of the poor light and poorer footing but because of his lingering aches and the awkward weight of the long-barreled Sharps. A Winchester would have been both lighter and more manageable, but the choice was not his.

Now he hunkered down with his back against a spire of rock, not merely for the support it offered but also to make sure he was not outlined against the morning sky, and waited.

He had no assurance that his plan would work. He knew he might spend the entire day here for nothing. But he had brought along a supply of smokes and several tins of meat. There was plenty of water flowing through the country at this time of year, so he did not have to worry about thirst if the wait was a long one. For that matter, up here there were still patches of ice-crusted snow under the trees and on the north sides of the huge boulders. He had climbed probably a thousand feet since leaving the cabin and was surprised at the amount of difference that made. There was much less grass here, and the aspens were all below him now. The trees were all conifers, and there was enough dry wood left from ancient blowdowns that a man could not use it all up in a lifetime of trying.

A fire would have been more than welcome, but he could not risk the chance that the smoke might be seen, so he hunched deeper into his coat and turned the collar up against the cold breeze that was coming off the tops of the surrounding peaks.

The sun crept slowly higher into the eastern sky and warmed him. By eight o'clock or so his coat was open and he was no longer shivering.

Somewhere around nine o'clock he heard the soft rattle of hoofs on stone reaching him from far below.

He set the Sharps aside and bellied down on the cold stone to look over the side of the abrupt drop.

Down below he could see a number of riders on the trail. They moved slowly.

Slocum grinned tightly and green fire danced in his eyes. The lead rider was Burl James. The acute overhead angle could not hide the man's bulk or the swaggering set of his shoulders as he rode at the head of the gold train.

Behind the riders came a line of laden mules.

Their packs all looked the same, but Slocum felt sure now that in some of those packsaddles would be the almost-pure gold taken from the vug somewhere deep inside the Beulah Four.

Down there, he was sure, was a fortune, destined either for Howard Rice and the men who worked his mine or for the pockets of Burl James and his gang of highwaymen.

It was Slocum's intention to make sure that gold went into Howard Rice's accounts. Even though the word in the camp that had reached him by way of Pearl was that there was a price on his head here, a price posted by Howard Rice and the Beulah Four.

Slocum still did not know for sure how Burl James

intended to accomplish his theft. But he knew how he would have done it, given the same set of circumstances and the same available manpower. He was banking on James having come up with the same idea.

He lay watching for a time, letting the mule train pass beneath him.

As he more than half expected, this time there were armed guards riding interspersed within the train of plodding mules. After every third mule there was a rider carrying a shotgun or a rifle across his pommel.

It was impossible from up here for Slocum to pick out the guards who had been with the Beulah Four for some time in the past and those James had imported for this job.

That fact angered Slocum—the fact that James's betrayal of Howard Rice gave the son of a bitch the excuse he needed to bring in his own men as an aditional guard force.

Worse, it had been James's adoption of Slocum's own robbery plan that was the impetus for the first aborted robbery that Slocum had foiled.

Still, if it had not been that plan that so neatly played into James's hands, there would have been some other. Slocum was sure of that now.

Those "guards" James brought in to beef up the security force had already been assembled and waiting, ready for the call to work. Obviously James had intended some kind of manufactured crisis even before Slocum came on the scene and threatened to disrupt his efforts.

Slocum grinned again. *My, oh my,* he thought, *isn't old Burl going to be surprised when he learns that the wanted outlaw John Slocum is not conveniently dead after all.*

Slocum slipped back away from the edge and picked up the Sharps. He looked at the rifle, not completely happy with it. In addition to the slower rate of fire in case he needed the weapon, he had not yet had a chance to shoot it. And factory sights with factory-range markings were only a starting point to determine actual points of aim. He simply could not be sure of the rifle's accuracy until he tried it, and he had not been able to risk the noise and commotion of sighting it in at a known range. He hoped that would not become a problem later.

There was no choice now, though. He hefted the Sharps and set out along the high rim at a brisk walk, keeping pace with the gold-laden mule train and following the trail far overhead.

He came to the third cut in the mountainside that the mules were following and had to skirt around the fan-shaped drop toward the trail. There he had to increase his speed to a woodsman's jog in order to keep abreast of the slow-moving mules.

He jogged on ahead a little way after he was able to return to the high rim and stopped to rest for a few minutes while the mules caught up with him.

Whatever James planned, Slocum was fairly sure it would not involve the use of a hidden ambush from any of the three cuts.

That plan was fine for the capture of a few sacks of gold concentrate, as Slocum had once intended, but it would hardly pay enough to justify the amount of manpower James had brought into this play. Besides, with the guards riding among the mules now, that plan would be quickly thwarted by any of the men who were loyal to their employer.

It had to be something else, Slocum thought. And he thought he knew what it would be. The proof would come at the far end of the trail, where it reached the relatively open country at the teamsters' shack. That was where Slocum expected Burl James to show his hand.

Slocum walked on, holding to the pace of the mules. He

skirted the sloping beginnings of the second and the first cuts and this time jogged on ahead of the train so he could be in position above the trail end when the pack train arrived there.

He was much higher now than he had been when he climbed up to observe when James shot the captured man, so there was less danger of being spotted.

Slocum found a nest of dark gray boulders to sit in, well protected there from gunfire and with a rock wall at his back to insure against his being skylighted. He was well ahead of the mule train now and took the opportunity to smoke a cigar before the guards came in view.

Then he emptied the .50-90 cartridges out of his pockets and laid them on the rock in front of him where they would be available under his hand if, or when, the shooting started. He leaned forward and satisfied himself that the same rock would serve as a rest for the heavy barrel of the Sharps.

He was in shadow here, and the air was cool without direct sunlight to warm him, but he peeled off his coat and folded it. He put it on top of the rock and laid the barrel of the Sharps on it. The coat would help minimize barrel vibration, which could destroy the accuracy of a rifle when something hard was used as a rest.

Satisfied that he had done everything he could, Slocum waited.

Within minutes, Burl James rounded the last point of rock far below and to Slocum's left. James wheeled his horse on the open ground and motioned the men following him to the side, where they would be out of sight of the men who were leaving the trail.

Slocum grunted to himself. So far, it was going exactly as he had expected. That first group of riders were all James's men. They had to be for the plan to work. But then it was the Beulah Four's security boss who was in charge of this robbery. Small details like that would be no trouble at all to arrange.

The first of the mules plodded onto the level ground and were turned toward the corral where both mules and the draft stock of teamsters supplying the camp were used to waiting.

Slocum ground out his cigar butt and leaned forward to see how James handled it. He wished he had some field glasses so he could see better. The men below were quite a distance away.

He rubbed at his eyes and stifled a yawn. With all the work he had had to do last night in preparation for this morning, he had gotten practically no sleep at all. And what little rest he did get was fretful and uneasy. He was feeling the responsibility for Howard Rice's fortune, and he was not accustomed to that. Used to being free and footloose, responsible only for himself, he was sure now that he would not be able to enjoy any venture that would place the weight of other men's livelihoods on his broad shoulders. He had to admire a man like Rice who could accept that burden without complaint, but Slocum did not want any part of a business that would put him in the same category.

The first three mules were out into the bowl where the trail to Howard's Tailings began, and now the first of the mid-train guards appeared. Burl James sat in full view of the trail and motioned the man forward, giving him an all-clear signal with a wave of his hand.

Probably, Slocum thought, the son of a bitch was smiling. It was too far away for him to see James's expression, but he could guess at it easily enough.

As soon as the guard turned into the bowl, out of sight

of following riders still on the slim ledge, he was covered by the other guards, their shotguns aimed toward his belly.

Easy enough now to see which guards belonged to whom, Slocum thought. Howard's men were being snapped up as soon as they appeared.

Burl James continued to sit his horse in view from the trail, motioning the Beulah Four men on with assurances that all was well.

Around the point of rock, where they could not be seen, two of James's men held the Beulah Four guards under their shotguns while a third covered the Beulah Four boys as they reached the bowl.

The mules, aimed in the general direction of the corral, took care of themselves, plodding routinely into the confinement and waiting there patiently while James continued to collect the crew that was loyal to Howard Rice.

Eventually the tail-end guards came into sight. They, too, were James's people. Six of them then, Slocum saw—and James himself.

It was clever enough. In the unlikely event that something went wrong and the loyal guards were somehow tipped to the plan, it would have been too late once they were on the trail, because both the front and rear guards were the robbery crew.

Now, Slocum figured, Howard's men would be herded into the shack and locked in there, possibly tied as well, and James and his crowd could gather up the mules and horses and disappear, immensely more wealthy than when they woke up this morning.

Slocum yawned and tried to rub the fatigue out of his grainy, burning eyes. As soon as James and his crowd were out of sight, Slocum could climb down into the bowl and release them. Then together they could go collect Mr. James and his companions.

The dull, distance-muffled boom of a shotgun brought him alert, and he peered down into the bowl below him.

More shotguns were blasting now.

Howard Rice's men, six good men, were cut down like stalks of wheat under a scythe.

Flame and smoke lanced out of the shotgun tubes of James and his robbers, and Howard Rice's guards died where they stood. It happened so quickly that they had no time to try to run or to fight.

The guards crumpled into a broken, red-splattered heap, and James's crowd reloaded and fired into them again.

Disgust and fearsome anger rose in Slocum's gorge. There was no need for that slaughter. It was a senseless abomination.

The bastards could have ridden away. There was no need to kill six good men.

The Sharps leapt to Slocum's shoulder. He took quick aim on Burl James's belt buckle and squeezed the trigger.

A man in front of James staggered and fell from his horse.

Son of a *bitch,* Slocum raged. The damn rifle was shooting low, even at this acute angle, which should have made it throw high if anything. The pre-marked sights were wildly inaccurate.

He threw the finger lever down, ejecting the spent shell casing, and grabbed up another cartridge from those laid out in front of him.

Jamming the fresh shell into the chamber and yanking the lever up again, he took aim a foot above Burl James's head and pulled the trigger.

There was no satisfying shove against his shoulder, no bellow of exploding powder.

"Bastard!" he screamed, both at himself and at Burl James. He had been carrying a Winchester for so long that habit had taken over, and he had forgotten that the damned Sharps only loaded with the lever. The hammer had to be cocked separately.

He earred the hammer back, but by then James had gotten over the shock of the unexpected attack and was spurring his horse toward the corral.

It was too far to try a shot at a running, bobbing target, so Slocum shifted his aim to a robber who was already at the gate, trying to get the mules lined out onto the trail. He squeezed the shot off, holding well over the man's head, and the robber toppled off his horse.

"Better, damn it," Slocum muttered.

He reloaded the Sharps, hands flying to perform the unaccustomed task, and cocked the rifle again.

James was at the corral gate now. Two of his men were inside the enclosure, herding the mules out onto the trail.

Slocum snapped a shot at James, but the man's horse was dancing and shifting, and the slug missed the big man. Slocum cursed and reloaded.

The mules were out now, and moving. Someone down below began firing uphill toward Slocum's protective nest of rocks.

He need not have bothered with the stone parapet. The distance was entirely too much for a scattergun. He never knew where the lead pellets fell, but it was nowhere near him.

Slocum fired again. Again James's shifting movement caused him to miss, and he cursed bitterly. He wanted Burl James. He wanted the man dead.

The mules were lined out away from the Howard's Tailings trail, the robbers slapping at them with slickers and quirts, trying to hurry them into a run. Several of the men persisted in trying to fire back at Slocum. Smoke from the Sharps had him spotted for them now. But he was in no danger at all from the shotguns. One of them tried potting him with a revolver, but he never heard that slug either. For long range the only weapon that would do any good at all would have been a rifle, and all of the rifles down there had been carried by the Beulah Four guards. There was no time for the robbers to go for any of those discarded weapons now.

Slocum managed to drop another of the robbers, but they were hurrying the mules down the wagon road now. Within seconds they were out of sight.

Slocum picked up his supply of .50-90 cartridges and shoved them into his pockets. He began hurriedly to scramble down the mountainside toward the slaughterhouse of dead men Burl James and his partners had created. Slocum moved quickly but with a deliberation born of the certainty that before this day was over, he was going to face Burl James. And cut the son of a bitch down.

He had no doubt at all that exactly that would happen. And he was looking forward to it.

19

Slocum paused at the foot of the slope to stand beside the dead men in silent apology. He had not anticipated this, or he would have done something to try to stop it. He had not known these men, but he had respected them, and they deserved better than Burl James had given them. He made a silent promise to avenge each one of them.

He heard the soft clatter of a hoof on rock, and the blued steel of the Colt appeared in his fist. A rider rounded the point of rock, coming from the direction of the camp.

"Howard!" Slocum said.

Howard Rice was carrying a Winchester rifle. It was cocked, and he aimed the barrel toward Slocum's stomach when he saw the revolver and the dead men tumbled together on the bloody ground.

Deliberately, Slocum let the hammer down on his Colt and dropped the revolver into his holster. "I'm sorry, Howard. I wasn't expecting this."

Rice looked past Slocum to the dead guards. His age-seamed face twisted in grief. "Your note, John. I didn't believe it. Lord help me, I didn't believe it. And I sent these men to their deaths." He uncocked the Winchester and shoved it into the scabbard under his leg. He swung down to the ground and led his horse nearer, anguish on his features. He looked old. "Are you sure . . . ?"

Slocum nodded. "James's men were all carrying shotguns. Your boys didn't have a chance, and I was too far away to help."

Rice looked around the bowl. The three robbers Slocum had shot lay there. There were also several loose horses cropping grass in the silence. The other saddle horses belonging to the dead men had been gathered up with the mules and ran with them when James and his men fled the bowl under Slocum's long-range fire.

"You did some good, John."

"Not enough."

"They likely have too much of a lead for us to catch them," Rice said. "I'll post a reward, of course. I'll put up my whole damn mine if that's what it takes. But I'd like you to help me, John. I'd like you to help me go after them, just as long and as far as it takes. I want to know that those men are brought to justice." The old man sighed. "If you are willing to return to my employ, that is."

"I never left you, Howard."

Rice rubbed the back of his neck. "No, I guess you didn't at that, John. Forgive me for doubting you. Please do that much for me."

"There's no forgiveness necessary, Howard. Given the same set of supposd facts, I reckon I'd have come to the same conclusions that you did. There's none of us can say he's never made a mistake. Or these boys wouldn't be dead now."

"We have to bury them. Or maybe it would be better to take them back to the camp, where they can be tended to with dignity."

Slocum shook his head. "We can do that later, Howard. We should do that, of course. But first we have to catch up with Mr. James so he can go back to Howard's Tailings too. Alive or dead. Preferably dead."

Rice gave him an odd look. "They surely have too much of a lead for us to hope to catch them. And once they reach the canyons down below, they could take any direction. It may not be possible for us to track them."

"They haven't gone far," Slocum said.

"Not far? But they must have left here quite a while ago."

"A half hour. Something like that."

"They will be miles down the road by now."

Slocum shook his head. "Not more than a mile I'd say. Probably less."

"But—"

"Last night, Howard, while Pearl was delivering my message to you, I slipped around and went into the Beulah Four's stables. Every mule you own has had its hooves sored, horseshoe nails driven into the quick.

"I hated to do that to the dumb brutes, but I figured it was the best way to keep the robbers from getting away. As long as the mules were kept at a walk they did all right, but as soon as James and his bunch tried to force them into a run those nails got bothersome. By now every mule in that train has balked and refused to move on, and I don't know of anybody that can make a mule do something that would hurt it that bad."

Slocum made a face. "I really am sorry about doing that to your stock, but they'll get over it. You'll need to give them good care, bring in a top-notch farrier if you don't have one, and they won't be worth much to you for the next month or so. But I can pretty much promise you that they haven't gone very far. As a matter of fact, I was planning to get these boys free and go after James on foot with them after he took off with the mules. I just didn't know he was going to do this."

"By God, John, the two of us can handle it."

"Are you sure you're up to it, Howard? I can take after them on my own. I mean, you're a mining man, not a gunfighter."

Rice snorted. "I wasn't always this age, boy. I was there when we went up the hill at Chapultepec. I've smelt my share of powder and heard the cannonballs fly. Cowardly sons of bitches like those up ahead turn my stomach, but they won't turn me back."

Slocum nodded. He laid the Sharps down and picked up one of the Winchesters the guards had carried. He had no idea where there might be any spare ammunition for the rifle, but the loaded magazine should be enough. He turned to fetch one of the loose horses, then paused and turned back to Rice.

"You were an officer, weren't you?"

"I was an officer," Rice admitted.

"Did you know the General, then?"

Rice had no difficulty understanding who it was that Slocum meant. "It was my privilege to campaign with Robert. We were classmates once."

"Then it is even more of an honor for me to ride at your side. Sir."

The old man and the younger rode together down the road, determination on their faces and rifles in their hands.

They found the outlaws three-quarters of a mile down the road, exactly as Slocum had predicted.

James and his three men had given up trying to get the mules to move forward. They were frantically trying to shift the sacks of gold from the mules to the horses that had come with them.

Foolishly they were trying to lash the sacks to the

saddles the horses already carried instead of shifting packframes onto the animals.

Slocum and Rice stopped in the shelter of a small grove of trees less than a hundred yards from the sweating and obviously frightened men.

"What do you say, John? How would you plan your attack?"

"I defer to your orders, sir. But if I were in command, I would give myself the pleasure of a charge."

Howard Rice gave him a thin-lipped smile. "Exactly what I had in mind myself, John."

"At your command, sir."

The old man cocked his Winchester and rammed steel to the flanks of his horse. A low, resonating whoop tore from his throat, quite unlike the high, raw Rebel yell that was ripped involuntarily out of Slocum.

Side by side the old warrior and the younger swept out onto the open ground in full view of their enemies.

A rifle attack from the protection of the trees would have been safer. Neither was interested in safety. They wanted to close with their enemy and smash them into the ground. Ride them down. Destroy them.

The robbers were confused by the unexpected charge. James and one of his men grabbed for their shotguns. The two others broke and ran.

Howard Rice rode tall in his stirrups, levering and firing as fast as he could work the Winchester's lever. Slocum was at his side, reins dropped over the horn, rifle spitting fire and death.

Two of the robbers went down in that first awesome volley from the charging horsemen.

The man standing beside James threw down his shotgun and tried to flee.

Slocum's Winchester was empty. He threw it aside and brought his Colt into the fight.

Burl James was immediately in front of him. Slocum saw flame blossom from the end of James's shotgun. He ignored it and snapped a shot into James's belly, then another.

His horse swept past the man, and Slocum fired down into James's body as the animal leaped over him. He hauled the horse to a stop, wheeled around, and shot the bastard again, regretting as he did so that James would not live long enough to be battered and beaten by Slocum's avenging fists as well.

Scant yards away, Howard Rice was still in full charge. The last of the robbers was tearing pell-mell down the empty road, leaving gold and guns and fallen companions behind.

Rice gave out another low, ripping war cry and spurred his horse straight at the robber.

The old man held his empty rifle like a war club or a saber. Apparently he did not have a pistol, or perhaps he simply preferred this combat.

The robber heard him coming and tried to dodge away from the flying, steel-shod hoofs of the charging horse.

Rice came even with him. The iron-plated buttstock of the Winchester was already slashing downward. It had to have been decades since Rice had practiced the stylized and formal strokes of the Dragoon saber, but his arm had lost neither its strength nor its skill.

The butt of the Winchester sliced unerringly down on top of the running man's skull.

The robber threw up an arm in a futile attempt to ward off the wicked stroke. The arm snapped. And then the polished wood swept through to find and to split his skull.

Rice yanked his horse down and spun it over its hocks, raising the shattered rifle for another, unnecessary stroke.

The old man was breathing hard, and there was the awful gleam of combat flaring in his eyes.

"Enough, Howard." Slocum rode over to him. Rice was still darting his head from side to side, puffing as hard as if he had just completed a long uphill race, looking for another enemy to destroy.

"Enough, Howard," Slocum repeated. "That's all of them."

"What? Oh." Rice calmed his horse and calmed himself. He looked at the broken Winchester, its stock reduced to splinters after the impact of the saber stroke, and looked puzzled, as if he could not remember what might have damaged the weapon. "Oh," he repeated.

"We'd better start gathering the horses, Howard, and putting the packs on them. The mules will have to stay here until they feel up to walking some more. And this carrion," he hooked a thumb toward the dead robbers, "can stay here, too. I figure it's only fitting that the buzzards have a meal off them."

Rice nodded and nudged his horse toward the patiently waiting mules, still piled high with gold and concentrate.

20

Slocum raised his glass and clinked it against Howard's. For this occasion he was willing to drink brandy with the old gentleman, even though he preferred the hard, clean bite of whiskey. "To your health, Howard. With my thanks."

"Stop that now, John. The thank-yous are all for me to give and you to receive. We won't go into that again."

"Well, you've been damn generous with me, Howard. I want you to know I appreciate it. I haven't been this thoroughly heeled in a long time." He grinned. "Never have been that I've gotten it legal, I reckon."

Rice chuckled. "Before you leave tomorrow, John, there is something I've been wanting to talk to you about."

Slocum was puzzled. Howard sounded hesitant, as if he was about to discuss something of great importance and did not know how to broach the subject.

Hell, Slocum thought, they had already talked it all out. Slocum would handle the security arrangements taking the gold shipment out in the morning. Mules—and, more important, trustworthy people—had already been located. And Rice had sent for a man he knew he could completely trust as his new chief of security after Slocum refused repeated offers of the job. Slocum's trip out this time would be one way only. Surely after all those refusals

Howard was not going to try again to convince Slocum to stay on in the tiny, isolated camp.

"Name it, Howard. We'll thrash 'er out."

"It's about . . . well, what I wanted to talk to you about is your young lady."

"Pearl?"

"Exactly," Howard said.

"What about her?"

"I was wondering if . . . well, if you intend to travel with her. I mean, I can well understand you wanting to keep her with you. But if, by any chance . . ."

Slocum threw his head back and began to laugh. That was the one detail he had not yet worked out. Maybe it was not going to be such a problem after all, trying to figure out how he could rid himself of the burden Pearl put on him.

Howard failed to find any humor in it, not understanding Slocum's reluctance to travel with another person he would have to look out for. "If I have offended you, John . . ."

"Of course you haven't, Howard. Do you like Pearl?"

The old gentleman gave him a shy smile and a nod.

"The gal *is* kinda good at what she does," Slocum said. "Which is why I sent her in here with that note. But there was another reason, too, my friend. I had already got the impression from your other ladies that you favored that sorta thing. And, you see, I just don't want to be saddled with a woman to watch over. Not in the places I sometimes travel. It wouldn't be healthy for her nor for me, either one. To tell you the truth, I was kind of hoping that you could find a place for her in your household."

"Do you mean that, John?"

"Damn right I do. I got no use for her. Between times, that is."

"But what can I give you?"

"You already have. Many times over. Just treat her decent, which I know you'd do anyway. Hell, she's had more than her share of hard knocks. It's about time the girl latched onto somebody who will be good to her. I can't think of anybody who'd be better for her."

Howard frowned. "It sounds perfect to me, but we shall have to ask her opinion of it."

Slocum shook his head. "She wouldn't understand that, Howard. I'll just tell her I've given her to you. That will satisfy her for the time being. Hell, it's the only way she'd understand right now. Later on you can teach her what it is to be a free and respectable person. She's got no idea of what that is yet, you know. It will take some getting used to, and you'll likely have to go about it slow, but you can do it."

"She has a great deal of potential, you know. Why, Lynnanne can teach the child so much."

Slocum grinned. "That Lynnanne could teach most *anybody* so much."

Howard chuckled. "Couldn't she, though?"

Slocum polished off the brandy and reached for a cigar. "It's getting kind of late, my friend. Would you mind if I turn in now? I want to be sharp tomorrow when we take your shipment out."

"Of course not, John." Howard stood and offered his hand. "I'll see you before you leave in the morning, of course, but I want you to accept my thanks once again." The old gentleman gave him a crooked, impish grin. "Sleep well tonight, John."

"Right." Slocum excused himself and went upstairs. He grumbled just a little when he discovered that Catherine had forgotten to light his bedside lamp. But he knew the room well enough by now that he did not bark his shins or knock anything over.

He found the bed and stripped, hanging the holstered Colt on the bedpost and crawling naked between the clean, fresh-smelling sheets.

The laundry must just have been done, he thought, and someone had added some kind of scent to the wash water because he sure could smell some sort of flowery stuff, almost like a perfume. Or several perfumes.

He stretched and plumped the down pillow up beneath his head.

Then he froze.

He could feel something . . . a warm something? . . . slowly creeping toward him.

Senses keenly turned, rigid with a readiness to fight if that was necessary, he tensed, his hand going toward the always-ready Colt.

He heard a low purr of contained laughter. And then another.

He was not alone in the darkened room. Someone else was there. Someone was laughing, or choking.

The sound seemed to come from several different places at once.

"What the hell . . . ?"

The laughter erupted around him. Feminine laughter. Women's voices. He was sure of that.

"Who the hell is here?" he demanded.

There was the laughter again. Then the brush of warm flesh against his and a slight shift of weight on the bed beside him.

"Guess," a woman's voice whispered in his ear.

Slocum grinned. "Catherine," he said. "I'd know that voice anyplace."

"No, darling John, I'm over here," came another whisper.

"And I'm down here." It was Pearl's distinctive tone, followed by a fit of giggles.

"And I am right here," the first voice said.

He was surrounded by the voices, and then by a seemingly endless sea of bare female flesh.

"All of you?"

The three of them went into gales of laughter.

"It was Howard's idea," one of them said.

"Dear Howard."

"It was a good idea."

"We approve of it."

Slocum could not begin to figure out which of them was saying what.

They all tumbled onto the bed with him, laughing and pressing themselves onto him, cuddling and fondling his balls, running fingers, lips, and tongues over him.

The fact was, Slocum decided, he did not *care* which of them was where.

He felt like he was drowning in a warm, moist flood of breasts and thighs, shaven pussies and hot, eager, slurping mouths.

He reached out and gathered them to him, reveling in the flow of flesh and sensation.

He really did not know which of them had the head of his bouncing tool in her mouth. Or which was nibbling along the length of his shaft. Or which was lapping wetly at his balls. He did not know, either, how the hell all three of them managed to squeeze into that confined area. He did not really care. He spread his thighs apart to give them more room to operate and let waves of exquisite pleasure wash through him.

Hot damn, he thought. *Lucky Howard. Lucky John.*

There was a clean, sweet-smelling pair of soft thighs nearby. He pulled the girl, whoever it was, over him and touched his tongue to her. She giggled and wriggled down closer onto him.

That sound might have come from Lynnanne, he thought. With a satisfied grin he realized it could just as easily have been made by Catherine or Pearl.

Poor Pearl. That was probably something she had never experienced. He thought about singling her out and teaching her about the pleasure a woman could receive from a man.

Unless perhaps he should leave that to Howard.

Unless perhaps he was *already* teaching her that.

He laughed, and the girl he was eating began to laugh. It was contagious. All of them began laughing, then roaring out loud, Slocum included.

He could feel three heads bobbing against his stomach and legs, and he could not stop laughing into the fresh-tasting crotch that was pressed against his face.

In the middle of it all, he felt completely unexpectedly the long, slow, sweet flow of come from his well-lapped cock, and whoever it was who had her lips wrapped around him lost her hold and got a face full of fluid.

Which only served to make them all laugh all the harder when she squealed out her dismay at having lost it.

That he was sure—well, *almost* sure—had been Lynn-anne's voice.

He felt some jostling down below as the girls pushed and shoved at each other, and one of the voices said, "My turn."

"No, mine," another returned.

"But I didn't get it right," one of the gigglers moaned.

"But it's *my* turn now."

They were all still laughing, though, so Slocum let the three of them scramble and scrap over him.

He lay back with a sigh, now and then flicking his tongue out, and enjoyed every marvelous moment of it.

Dawn, he thought with great pleasure, was a long, long time away. And he had sure made hard rides after longer periods without sleep.

He did not think he had ever found better reason to spend a night without slumber.

As content as he could ever remember being, John Slocum wriggled his hips and let the good feelings wash over, under, around, and through every part of him.

JAKE LOGAN